A Part of the Sky

Robert Newton Peck

A Part of
the Sky

Alfred · A · Knopf　New York

1994

THIS IS A BORZOI BOOK
PUBLISHED BY ALFRED A. KNOPF, INC.

Copyright © 1994 by Robert Newton Peck

Library of Congress Cataloging-in-Publication Data
Peck, Robert Newton.
A part of the sky / by Robert Newton Peck.—1st ed.
p. cm.
ISBN 0-679-43277-9
1. Teenage boys—Vermont—Fiction. 2. Farm life—Vermont—Fiction. 3. Shakers—Vermont—Fiction. 4. Family—Vermont—Fiction. I. Title.
PS3566.E254P3 1994
813'.54—dc20 93-41741
CIP

Manufactured in the United States of America
First Edition

ALSO BY ROBERT NEWTON PECK

A Day No Pigs Would Die

Path of Hunters

Millie's Boy

Soup *(a series)*

Fawn

Wild Cat

Hamilton *(a picture book)*

Hang for Treason

Rabbits and Redcoats

King of Kazoo *(a musical)*

Trig *(a series)*

Last Sunday

The King's Iron

Patooie

Eagle Fur

Basket Case

Hub

Mr. Little

Clunie

Secrets of Successful Fiction

Justice Lion

Kirk's Law

Banjo

Fiction Is Folks

The Seminole Seed

Dukes

Spanish Hoof

Jo Silver

My Vermont I

My Vermont II

Hallapoosa

The Horse Hunters

Arly

Arly's Run

Higbee's Halloween

*To a mother and aunt
who worked a farm as men
yet stayed softer than quilts.*

A Part of the Sky

Chapter

I

"Robert," he said, "thank you for coming on time."

I smiled. "You can bank on me, Ben. Just as you could always count on my father."

"Punctuality is a Vermont virtue. Perhaps our only."

Mr. Benjamin Franklin Tanner, our neighbor, returned his watch to a pocket and held out a hand. Ben's handshake was firm yet friendly. Together we walked toward Mr. Tanner's freshly whitewashed horse barn.

"No school today?"

"Yes, but I don't go too regular. I like school a lot. And my teachers. But we somehow got to keep our home. So the eighth grade can possible do without me."

Mr. Tanner understood. My father, Haven Peck, died two weeks ago; I'd skipped school a few days to work our farm, taking over for Mama and Aunt Carrie. Ben didn't scold. I had choices to make. And made them.

We stopped in the long aisle outside a box stall where a stallion smell was male strong. It was seven o'clock on a May morning, so I had to squint to see beyond the stall bars. Inside, a powerful horse turned to stare at us. His name, neatly lettered on the gate shingle, read:

GENERAL ROBERT E. LEE

"This big gentleman might turn a lick frisky," Ben warned, sliding the door a foot, "so best we don't spook him. Easy boy," he told his chesty gray.

"He's right handsome," I said. "Always is."

General nickered.

Pulling a carrot from a shirt pocket, Ben Tanner snapped off a short orange log, offering the treat on his open palm. General Lee sniffed it, approved, lipped and munched. As he ate, Ben touched the stud's massive neck with a cautious hand, then slipped a well-oiled halter over head and ears, fastening the buckle tongue to a snug but comfortable notch.

"Now then, Robert, let's parade him out into the morning where I can see to check him over,

— 4 —

to certain that he's sound. Mr. Haskell Gamp's coming at ten o'clock and bringing a wet mare."

We led General from his stall to a work area, a wide doorway that looked up to the main house.

"Here'll do," Ben told me.

Raising a hoof, General rapped the thick oak floor with his iron, making a hollow sound like a drum.

"Our friend knows something's up." Ben winked at me. "Perhaps he reckons he's fixing to entertain a lady visitor. That's the reason he wasn't free in the meadow last night. I boxed him so he'd behave quieter."

While I gripped the halter strap with a firm ten-finger purchase, Ben Tanner patted the gray withers, his hand floating softly and slowly, to inform General of his exact location and friendly intentions.

Bending low, he hefted a front hoof.

"Around any horse, Rob, be it familiar or strange, it'll usual serve best to fetch up a front leg first. Even if you purpose to tend aft. Working with an animal's brain saves time and sweat. A carrot'll do ample more than a whip or a nose twitch."

"Papa said such," I agreed. "He killed hogs, but he had a gent's way about him."

Looking up at me, our neighbor offered a sad smile. "Indeed. I truly miss Haven Peck. So does Bess."

It was sort of magical. Because hardly had Ben Tanner spoke his wife's name, she appeared, walking toward us in a pink-and-white apron, carrying a glass of something in each hand.

"Morning, Mrs. Tanner," I said, although I'd been told to use their first names.

"A morning to you, Rob," she said with a smile. "Now, the pair of you, don't start thinking you're royalty. I'm cleaning out the cooler, and I happened to have two glasses of buttermilk in the way. So here you go. Partake."

Ben downed his, I mine. It tasted rich and right restful. Bess wiped a corner of my mouth with a clean hanky and returned it to her apron pocket. As we handed our empty glasses to her, she took them with a wry face.

"The trouble with buttermilk," she said, "is that the empty glass looks so untidy."

"Thanks," I said. "Thanks a lot."

Ben nodded. We watched her amble back toward her kitchen, a dirty glass in each hand. Ben stood there holding his gray stallion until his wife disappeared inside the house. "At times," he said softly, "I treasure Bess so much that it's all I can do to keep from letting her know it."

He moved slowly to the stallion's rear, maintaining contact, his shoulder brushing General's furry flank. Winter was still thick on him, along with stall dust.

"How's his hoofs?" I asked.

Stooping, Ben grunted. "Three appear solid. Now let's handle number four." Cradling the hoof between his knees, Ben used his thumbnail to chip off a few brown clods of dried mud. "Frog's firm. The inside rim of the hoof feels soft and moist. That's a blessing. Hard hoofs make a hard-hearted horse." He paused. "But his shoe begs a reset."

Ben left, returning with smithing tools. Under his armpit was a short fullering bar. In seconds, he loosened the problem shoe and pried it off. The iron fell clanking to the wood.

"Will we use a fire?" I asked.

"No need. Were I to attend him fresh footwear, I'd shoe hot. No other way."

It made me almost grin to remember. Papa wouldn't trust any farrier who would shoe cold. A mare was a lady who deserved warm slippers on her feet. I could hear Papa teaching me. I'd never forget any of his earthy reason. I carried his lessons with me, hurting like a pebble in a boot that I'd never empty out.

Whack. Whack. Whack.

The noise of Ben Tanner's hammer brought me back to where I was now standing, steadying my neighbor's stallion.

Releasing the hoof, Ben straightened up slowly with a groan of age. "There," he said, "he's repaired. But before I twist off those nail points, cast your young eyes down yonder and lend me your opinion."

As Ben held the halter, I squatted to raise the hoof. It felt solid set. Even all around. "Snug tight," I said. Before rising, I discovered a few brown burdock burrs on General's fetlock. Small ones. Placing my free hand on the pastern, to steady the leg, I eased off the burrs. Then I stood.

"Robert, you have a genuine touch for animals. That's why I asked you to help me with my stud horse. You do possess a Peck manner. A quiet Shaker way." Ben clapped a hand on my shoulder. "Never had I ever see a human being, man or boy, tame a pig the way you done last summer. That Pinky of yours, formerly mine, was close to a household pet."

I nodded. "My mistake was giving her a name."

"A shame you and your pa had to butcher Pinky. She was barren. Her end was a sorrow for you, Robert. Yet rightful and proper." Ben sighed. "Manhood is doing what has to be done."

Remembering that dreadful December day, I realized that Papa had also killed a part of himself. Ben knew all about it. Said so. He and Bess meant a lot more to me than just neighbors. I ached to thank him, but I never seemed to find the right words.

Before I could say anything, General Robert E. Lee tossed his mighty head twice, and rumbled his throat.

"This boy must've took a whiff of something he didn't like," Ben said. Looking at me sideways, he asked, "You been breakfasting to beans?"

Laughing, I pleaded innocent. "No, just some of Mama's chicken giblet stew, spoon bread, vinegar, and turnips."

"Hold him steady," Ben said, "while I fuller that hoof to prosperity."

Using tongs, he twisted off a silvery nail spike that was prickering up through the hoof, and bit off a second. He'd barely finished ironing when the stallion set to prancing his legs up and down, and I couldn't manage to settle him.

"Whoa," I whispered. "Whoa now, General."

Ben stood. "Horse, what's got into you? There's not a bother of anything to smell."

As he spoke, I sudden knew that Mr. Ben Tanner was dead wrong. Looking downroad, I spotted a horse and rider coming our way at a trot. I noted a bridle but no saddle; the horseman seemed to sit unsteady as he bounced along, feet pointing out on both flanks of the horse as though he weren't too comfortable at riding. He rode stiff-legged.

"Somebody's coming, Ben."

The stallion wouldn't hold still. He persisted his dancing, snorted, and shook his mane. His tail arched as he fluttered a louder noise in his throat. A bear of a sound.

"Hold him, Robert. Help me."

It was hard to believe that somebody would actual ride a wet mare toward a stud. Yet this man rode closer, trying to contain his mount. It was a bay. A deep brown with a black mane and tail.

"Dang!" Ben spat. "It's Haskell Gamp. That uppity man never could tell time, even if'n you painted a clock on his face. I particular asked him not to appear until ten o'clock, so's I could afford General some extra oats and plenty of water to humor him down."

When the mare nickered, trouble exploded.

There was no holding General Lee, now that he could see and hear a heated female he'd earlier caught wind of. Nostrils flaring, he reared high, boxing the air with his front hoofs. Ben tried to cling to the halter. His legs and my legs left the ground as I heard the halter snap. The gray stallion busted free.

As my hands clawed and clutched at the mane of the rearing horse, the stud bucked, wheeled away from me, and attacked his owner. Ears back, he bared his teeth, then bit deep into the flesh of Ben's body, between his neck and shoulder. Ben Tanner's mouth opened, but the force of those long and powerful horse jaws silenced his scream.

The gray, with his teeth planted into human meat, shook Ben worse than a terrier shakes a rat. Blood splattered.

What eased Ben was because a in-season mare was present. As the stud charged her, Mr. Gamp fell off. On the ground, he lay yelling for help among eight active hoofs, his hands trying to protect his face from the dust and danger. When a stallion and a mare are both eager, it's more ruckus than romance. Nature's violent way.

Kneeling to Ben, I watched it all happen.

As General was trying to smell the bay's rump, she kicked at him. Below, Mr. Gamp still held one of the bridle reins, and screamed. Above him, the two horses madly circled, ears back, around and around. Wild-eyed, the stallion was trumpeting, grunting, his hind legs spread and braced. Underneath him, he was extended, rigid, trying to gain position. Soon his teeth found her neck, clamped, and held. The mare's neck arched, her head twisting one way and then another in an effort to escape the pain.

General was larger, stronger, and not to be denied his stallionhood. As the bay began to tire, General dominated her with his superior weight, strength, and desire.

The stud mounted the mare, had his way, and their unity ended as sudden as it had begun. The animals shuddered, froze for a breath, then parted. Both become docile.

A dusty Mr. Gamp rose slowly to his feet to stagger to where Ben lay bleeding. Ben Tanner's shirt, what little of it hadn't been ripped off, was soaked dark with blood. Skinning off my own shirt, I quickly wadded it to a bundle, then pressed it against the gushing wound, pushing the soft cloth to Ben hard as possible.

After a spell, his bleeding slowed and clotted. Gamp did little except stand there, whining, eyes red and face flushed. A dirty mess of a man. Fear flooded his face. As he leaned close, his breath was sour as sin. Removing a pint bottle of whiskey from his pants pocket, and backing away, he uncorked it with his teeth to gulp a swallow.

Then a second.

To me, it become clear that Mr. Gamp had probable been halfway to mellow when he'd arrived on his mare. So, standing up, I walked to him, took the bottle from his trembling fingers, and poured the remaining whiskey to the Vermont soil. There was a temptation in me to throw that bottle away, as far as I could pitch it. Or smash it. Yet I did neither. I merely handed it back to Mr. Gamp, so he'd keep it for a time.

I hoped he would remember this day, and how much hurt he'd heaped on a good man.

Chapter

2

"More beans?" Mama asked me.

My mother, Aunt Carrie, and I were sitting at our kitchen table, at supper. On the big black Acme American six-griddle cookstove, a pot of beans was always simmering on a back burner. When times were easier, there was usual a hunk of sowbelly or fatback in the bean pot, for flavor. But lately, there didn't seem to be more than beans to eat. Or dandelion greens.

"Please," I said, "if we can spare it. Let's all have some."

Neither my mother nor my aunt spooned a second helping to their plates. It wasn't because they weren't hungry. Both of them would have starved to prosper me.

At noon, a meal we Vermonters called dinner, Mama often prepared cold baked-bean sandwiches between generous slabs of her homemade bread. For years, I'd toted those to school. Few offered to trade their sandwiches for mine, yet it didn't bother me a mite. I was proud of whatever Mama stirred on her stove.

Maybe the kids at school were just plain too jealous of me to trade. That was my secret smile.

Earlier, at the Tanner place, I'd ducked my shirt under the pump to rinse away Ben's blood. Bess had offered to wash it for me. But I thanked her and said there was no need. Mama had made the shirt herself, as she cut and stitched all of my clothes. Kids at school said things about that too, noticing that my shirts were plainer than my eats. We Shakers were Plain People. We needed no frills on our backs or on our plates.

As I forked in hot beans, Mama and Aunt Carrie seemed to be eyeing my shirt. I smelled questions in the oven. So I squeezed off the first shot.

"No, I didn't go to school today. I hiked over the hill to Ben's, to help him with his stud horse."

"So," said Aunt Carrie, in her churchy tone, "you missed your schooling again."

"I'll go soon."

Pulling a dollar from out of my pocket, I unfolded it, giving it to Mama. "I earned a dollar. Ben likes my work."

Mama didn't reach out to take it, so Mr. George Washington just lay there on the gray boards, as wrinkled and tired as I felt.

"Robert," said my mother, "please go to school tomorrow."

"No, not tomorrow. Even though I want to."

"How come?" Mama asked me.

"Well, not because I dislike school in general. I take to most all of it. Except for this guy called William Shakespeare. In English class, we only got one book, so we have to take turns standing up front and reading a play that doesn't make a speck of sense to me. It's called *As You Like It* . . . and I don't like it."

Mama smiled.

Aunt Carrie held her ground.

"Mr. Shakespeare, for my opinion, ought to title his play *As You Hate It*. I'd be pleasured to give him that idea, for free. The teacher I like so much, Miss Malcolm, told us he died. But if *he* had to stand up in English class and read that stuff out loud, you'd know what did him in."

My mother laughed. "What's the play about?" she asked.

"Well," I said, chewing my beans, "it isn't about anything . . . except two brothers, Oliver and Orlando. They're fixing to sweet up their girlfriends,

Celia and . . . and Rosie. Their main hobby is gallivanting around Mr. Arden's Forest and touching stones. In fact, this guy Touchstone is also a Chester. On top of all that, there's a Frederick guy who I think has a dog named Duke."

"My," said my mother, "for a boy who doesn't attend school regular, you've near to mastered it all."

Hearing her praise swelled out my chest an inch. Or maybe it was bean gas.

Tomorrow, I had already decided, *As You Like It* would have to limp along through Arden's woods without me. No time to quit doing for Ben Tanner. Today had been bad on him.

After Mr. Haskell Gamp collected his settled mare and led her in the direction of town, toward Learning, Bess Tanner and I tended her husband. The wounds bled clean. Yet it was plain that Ben needed sewing. But before she threaded her needle, Mrs. Tanner smacked us with a surprise.

It was hard liquor.

Bess, I knew, was a solid and fearing Baptist, a white-ribbon lady who didn't partake or approve of spirits. So, when Bess fetched a glass jug of mountain white, colorless as water, uncorked it, and offered a pull to her husband, I near fainted to her kitchen floor.

"Drink up, Benjamin," she said. "Because the Almighty won't expect you to take sober stitching. And neither do I."

Ben drank. I did not. It was certain a shocker to see him do it, because Ben Tanner was as hard-shelled a Baptist as Learning could boast of. Tough hide and tender heart. His woman told him to put himself outside of a second swallow, and he lightened the jug again. Then she placed the handle of a wooden cook spoon crosswise in his mouth.

"Bite," said Bess. "Bite it deep."

As he sat in a kitchen chair, Ben nodded that he was ready for iodine and thread. And, stitch after pulled-tight and knotted stitch, he bore it as I knew he could. One by each.

Silently, as I held Ben to the chair, I counted the stitches. He took thirty-seven without a whimper. And I knew it hurt Bess more to piece him together. His white hair was sweaty wet, a shoulder now stained brown with iodine, his face reddened with the pain.

"You're not much," Bess whispered to him as she tied the final, "but you're all I got."

When his wife removed the foamy spoon from his mouth, Ben looked at her, and asked a question in a trembling voice. "Bess, would you please forgive me if I let out a cuss?"

Touching his face, Bess said, "If this embroidery of mine doesn't pardon swearing or whiskey, I don't know whatever do. Cut it loose."

With her red and shiny hands, Bess Tanner covered *my* ears instead of *hers*. That was when Ben fired off a masterpiece of low language for near to half a minute, without repeating a single sorry word. Nothing new or real fancy. Just a steady string of old favorites.

"Feel better?" she asked him.

Forcing a grin, Ben nodded. "It wouldn't been so bad," he said to his wife, "except that I always knew how you enjoy needlework."

Bess faked a frown.

The next chore took a spell longer. With Bess under one arm, and me (shirtless) beneath the other, Ben Tanner stumbled upstairs to his bed. We pulled off his boots, stockings, and bloodstained trousers, and eased him careful, reeking of iodine, to a pile of pillows.

Bess paid me a dollar.

All this I told to Mama and Aunt Carrie. As they listened without a word, their faces turned serious and spoke how sorry they were that a bad thing had happened to such a sturdy neighbor.

When I come to the part about the stitches, Mama touched my arm, recalling, as did I, how

Ben Tanner's cow, Apron, tore me up about a year ago trying to drop her calf. Ben had found me and hauled me to home. Afterward, he give me a young pig, Pinky, for birthing a calf out of Apron.

"Will he be all right?" Mama asked.

I nodded. "Mr. Tanner's harder than a rock maple. So I figure he'll mend and be up and about. But until, best I help out some. A dollar a day is useful bank money. There's work here to handle as well. Please . . . please don't nag or fret me about school. That ol' schoolhouse will be standing long after Ben Tanner's put to prone."

Mama said, "You can't do it all, Rob."

"No, s'pose not. But I'll swallow a slab of it. We have to keep our farm. Compared to Mr. Tanner's spread, ours isn't so much to look after. All we have is five acres. Not quite that, according to what Papa told me. But it's *ours*. And in four more years we'll own it outright, if'n we keep up payments to the Learning Bank. So stuff that dollar in the teapot."

"We'll help," Aunt Carrie said. "Your mother and I will do and do and do." She turned to her younger sister. "Won't we, Lucy?"

Mama nodded. "If we try our best, angels can do no better."

I took their hands. They felt small yet strong as

spruce. There was bark aplenty on my two little ladies.

"Say," I said, "it's time for a laugh. We agreed we'd have a good giggle every day. And believe me, I got one to share."

Mama smiled. "I could use a chuckler."

"It was something Ben Tanner said, just after Mr. Gamp left with his mare. Ben was lying there in the dirt. He got to his feet and helped me box General back in his stall. His face was twisted like taffy. So I asked him a dumb question about what it felt like to be bit so hard by a horse."

"What did he say?" Mama asked. "That is," she added with a wink, "if you can repeat it in front of Shaker ladies."

"I'd asked . . . *did it hurt?* And all Ben said was . . . *it gits your attention.*"

Chapter

3

Soon as I touched her teats, I knew that I wouldn't be getting very much. Nary a drop.

"Daisy," I told our milk cow, "you're drying up."

It was her usual morning milking time. Five o'clock. For a week now, Daisy's bag become smaller and softer. A time had passed since she'd dropped her last calf. Daisy was no longer young. The worry that she mightn't again freshen nagged at me.

Standing up, I patted our Holstein's warm side. "It's all right, old girl. You done us plenty for years. You've give. And allowed us to sell all your calfs for bank money."

Kicking the milking stool to one side, then dousing the lantern, I rinsed out the pail under the yard pump and hung it to its nail. Then I broke open the stanchion to turn Daisy back out to meadow.

Walking toward the house, I felt shameful that there'd be no milk for Mama's coffee, or for Aunt Carrie's. They would have to suffer it black. Ahead of me, a frail yellow lantern light in the kitchen said that both women were up, stoking the stove, fixing breakfast. I hoped it'd be fried apples and corn bread. Over my shoulder, I looked back to our little gray barn. How would we afford another cow? We should've kept Daisy's last calf. But it got sold off before Papa died, for ten dollars; part of the bank payment. Into Mama's teapot.

After breakfast, I went out to the meadow to fetch Solomon, our Holstein ox. Like usual, he grazed near Daisy.

"Come on, Solomon. It's May. The ground's free of frost, so today you and I have to turn the cornfield soil for seeding."

Leading him to the barn was no problem, as my hand on one curving horn was all it took. Our ox was as gentle as he was burly. Even though he weighed closer to two tons than one. About 3200 pounds.

I couldn't remember a time without Solomon. He was always there, working, sweating, leaning to his single yoke without fit or falter. Solid as barn timber, and more oak than animal. With a shrug of my shoulders, I don't guess I could imagine his age. Close to twenty.

Yoked, our big black-and-white ox coasted the plow on its side with no effort, as it was sliding along easy on the dewy meadow grass. In the early morning light, tiny silver spider webs lay every few feet. It was like looking down at a starry sky. Crop ground wasn't meadowland. Meadow was pasture; its turf was a green quilt of short mounded grass for grazing. But crop acres lay brown and barren, freckled by last season's corn stubble, like a man needing a shave.

Solomon stood patient while I righted the plow to set the blade. Beneath my bare feet, the ground felt damp, soft, and yielding.

Papa said the earth was a loving woman who wanted seed. Kneeling, I picked up a clod of moist loam and balled it. The soil smelled cool and friendly. Even though it dirtied my hands, as a Shaker I truly respected it; so many ways it fed our family.

Other than almost two acres for hay, we had two acres to plow for a field-corn crop, silage, so plowing didn't use better than five or six hours of steady work. From a six o'clock first light until noon.

Solomon pulled. Behind his mighty hindquarters, the silvery plowshare swam through the brown land smooth as a shiner fish. To help guide Solomon, I did something more'n unusual; I fixed a brace of long black-leather reins to the outer tips of his yoke, right and left, and tied the two loose ends behind my back. There was no way to grip them. Both my hands had to guide the curved plow handles.

For forward motion, I barked out a "Hup" to pull, and a "Ho" to whoa him. Like any trained Vermont ox, Solomon would "Gee" right, and "Haw" left.

Yet that wasn't all Solomon understood. Papa always claimed that he was as wise as King Solomon in our Bible. For me, Solomon seemed to know what to do and how to do it, and suffer the added chore of breaking in a clumsy boy for a workmate.

"Last row," I later told him under a high sun.

Solomon snorted, as if to say he blessed the idea of a noonday feed with a yoke off, beneath a meadow elm. Some farmers don't unyoke at noon. Papa always did. He said it was a Shaker's way, to honor work and all workers. Maybe that was the cause that we Pecks seemed as dear to Solomon as he was to us.

But we didn't quite complete the final furrow.

Solomon stopped and wouldn't budge. "Yup," I commanded him. No response. So I repeated the order in a louder voice, trying to make my thirteen years sound something like Papa's sixty. "Heeeee-yup!"

Solomon didn't take another step.

Instead, he mere lowered his head, as though the yoke was sudden too weighty to heft, and fell. Turning loose of the plow handles and then slipping out of the leather rein loop, I hurried to where his big head rested on the yet unplowed ground. He was alive, still breathing, but I sudden realized that old Solomon wouldn't be pulling a plow, or a wagon, another inch. The ox's eyes were open. But then, looking closer at them, I saw the graying clouds of winter, and age.

Solomon was near to blind.

Once, and only one time, he turned his soft face toward me, as if to tell me that he was sorry not to finish the furrow. Hurriedly, I yanked out the pair of cotter keys, loosened the bow, and pulled the heavy yoke off his neck. Slowly, barely moving, his proud head lowered to the ground as if to grace its goodness. One deep breath, and then nothing more.

I forgot about my plowing.

— 26 —

All I could make myself do was kneel in the dirt and hold his giant head close to my sweaty-wet shirt. His heat matched the late morning.

"Solomon." I whispered his name very softly, as if spoken to a violet, so that only God could hear. There was no way to know if oxen have souls. But if any ox did, it was Solomon. Touching him, stroking the sweaty curls on his massive head, I wanted to tell him that to have worked with him wasn't a task. It was a privilege.

Looking to my left, I could see our little gray shack of a house. Home. Yet inside, Mama and Carrie would be fixing dinner, for noon, and then coming outside to locate me. They'd see us here for certain. But I couldn't allow that, because the sight would hit them too hard.

I ran. Up, over the hill, all the way down to Mr. and Mrs. Tanner's big, prosperous farm, to pound at their front door with a mud-stained fist. Mrs. Tanner answered my knock. The door opened. She read my face.

"Rob," she said. "What is it?"

"It's our ox," I panted. "Solomon's down. And I can't abide having Mama or Aunt Carrie see him lying so still and turning cold. They both knowed him a spate longer than they knowed me. So, if it's all right with you, I'd like to yoke up your two and borrow 'em long enough to drag Solomon off into the trees, out of sight. I can shovel a hole for him, then cover him up proper, under earth. May I please?" I sucked in a breath. "Please. Before all the flies and ants and crows come to peck at him."

However, before Bess Tanner could answer me, it hit me that I'd failed to ask about Ben, and how he was mending.

"Manners," I heard Papa's voice tell me. "A man begins with his manners."

It was one of his longest sermons. Haven Peck was hardly a man of many words. Yet, at the rare moments he spoke, people (meaning me) seemed to listen up and record it.

"How's Ben?" I asked Bess, sounding like a feeble apology.

"More ornery than a wet cat," Bess said. "If you'd cotton to brighten my day, don't mention his name. He's the most unpatient patient that Satan ever afflicted." Bess sighed. "Enough of that. I'm sorry about your ox. Now then, will you be able to yoke Bob and Bib by your lonesome?"

"Yes," I said, "I have to."

"Come," she said, heading for their barn. "I'll show you where the yoke is. And," she paused, "perhaps lend you a hand. Their new yoke is solid hickory. Ben could barely manage it himself, and you know he's sturdy as a lumber-camp outhouse."

We almost trotted.

"Rob, go out meadow and bring the oxen in. Remember now, Bob's always to the left. Bib right. If you lead 'em, that's how. Walk between 'em and they'll respond comfortable. Hear?"

"I hear."

On the grass of meadow pasture, oxen will usual stand in the same fashion they pull. Bob, I figured, was grazing with Bib, his twin, on his right. Neither was full-out growed, but at over a year, both be ample large. Bob slightly blacker. They knew me. After all, the first pull in Bob's life was when, up on the ridge, I'd pulled him out of Apron's rump.

Bess helped me yoke, and locate a long metal drag chain. Thanking her, I headed her oxen up and over the ridge to our farm.

It took time. Papa once said, "When a man tries to hurry oxen, he only hurries hisself."

Mama and Carrie beat me to where Solomon lay cooling. Both of them were stooping near to him, to touch him a good-bye.

"I'm sorry you had to witness him," I said.

Mama nodded. "Soon's we did, Carrie and I reasoned where you'd gone to, and why."

It wasn't an easy pull for Bob and Bib, because of Solomon's mature size. Yet the two young Holsteins did for me, willingly, with little urging. We only had two shovels. But my mother and aunt turned stubborn about Solomon's grave and wouldn't allow me to dig lonesome. We took turns. You'll never see women work earth as they done that day.

Nobody spoke.

The three of us dug in a silent acceptance.

Then, after Ben's oxen dragged Solomon at and into the hole, we spaded dirt over him, adding two crossed twigs for a marker.

But we couldn't turn our backs on the grave and walk out of our little woods. The May afternoon seemed so quiet, as if adding its own silent psalm. A thrush warbled from high in a red-budding maple. The three of us held hands, dirt and all. Their fingers felt gritty in mine. Frail strength.

Daisy, I was facing up to, might die next. But this weren't no proper moment to tell my mother and her older sister.

As we stood by the massive mound of earth, Mama, in a quiet voice, spoke a few Shaker words about how farmers and animals live together, and die together on a shared plot. She recited it all like a hymn that was missing its music.

"The resting of death," Mama said, "becomes a part of the land, as clouds are a part of the sky."

Chapter

4

"Sit still," my mother ordered.

"I don't need a haircut. Not tonight."

Our kitchen was supper hot. Stuffed into Mr. Tanner's black church shoes and Will Henry's outgrowed blue suit (a gift), I felt hotter.

"And do stop scratching yourself," said Aunt Matty, who had come to help prepare me for battle. "You'll disturb the lice."

"It's my underwear. It itches like it's alive and crawling. Going to this dance weren't *my* idea. Becky Lee Tate promised me that if I took her, she'd somehow coach me so's I won't flunk English."

Years ago, Papa had warned me, "Never go into a kitchen where women are canning." Well, these three women were doing worse, making me boil like a clamped mason jar of processing peas.

Behind me, clicking her sewing scissors at my thatch of hair, Mama sighed. "Your first dance."

"Wrong. My last. I could throttle Will Henry for outliving these duds. Maybe I ought to stand out in a cornfield and play a scarecrow. Besides, I've never danced a step. So I hope Becky is wearing shin guards and hard-toe mill shoes."

Mama said, "It'll test her courage."

I winced.

"You'll have fun," Mama said, snipping another lock so it would fall inside my collar.

"Will ought to be taking her. After all, it's sort of his suit. Or used to be. I bet that Grange Hall will be hotter than the Devil's drawers."

Aunt Matty, who wasn't really my aunt, snickered. Aunt Carrie (who was) didn't. Mama pinched my ear.

"Robert," she said, "enough of that kind of talking."

"Sorry, ladies. It's because my shirt is already sweaty, and I haven't danced a square inch. Mama, do you *have* to chop my hair? Nobody's going to notice."

"Miss Becky might."

"Stand up," said Aunt Carrie, approaching me, "so I can right your necktie."

"What's wrong with it?"

"Well," she said, fussing at me, "you've got the little end hanging lower than the big end. And your knot's too bashful."

"Bashful?"

"Yes. The knot's trying to hide underneath one of your collar points. It's too loose. Here, I'll snug it up."

"You're choking me. How'll I ever kick up a polka, or whatever, if I can't breathe?"

"For somebody short of breath," Mama told me, "you certain say more than vespers."

There I stood, working up a fever, shifting my weight from one borrowed shoe to the other, with Aunt Carrie tugging my tie, and Mama behind, whacking away at my hair. Aunt Matty circled us in a supervising manner, like a cat ready to spring. All this, plus one more worry.

"Golly, maybe Becky is going to recognize Will Henry's suit. Suppose she does? I'll die."

"Now, now," said my mother. "If she's a lady, Becky Lee won't notice. But if she happens to, she won't let on, or bother."

"Never did I figure," I said, "that a dance is

worse than a dentist." I moaned. "Will's a good dancer."

"That'll be helpful," said Mama, examining a loose button on my sleeve. "Quite helpful."

"How so?"

"Because his suit is used to being graceful, no matter who's inside. So, forget your feet, and allow Will's talented pantlegs to guide you."

Her joke made us smile.

Meanwhile, below me on her knees, Aunt Matty stuck another pin in my leg and my trouser cuff. "Your socks don't match," she said. "You're wearing one blue and one green. Yes, I know. You have another pair just like these. And your pants could be let down at least two more inches. They look as if a flood's coming."

I grunted. "I ought to go naked."

"Good idea, Robert," my mother said. "With no clothes on, nobody'll notice you at all. Except the constable."

"All I'm lacking," I said, "is a sign on my back that reads . . . *If you have any gripes on this suit, tell 'em to Will Henry*."

For some reason, all four of us laughed.

"At last," said Mama, slipping her scissors to an apron pocket, "you're neat and tidy as President Hoover. I think you are final ready."

— 35 —

"Better be. Becky and Mr. Tate are coming to fetch me in their Ford. So I best not keep 'em waiting."

"Rob," asked Aunt Matty, "do you remember what I taught you, about dancing?"

"Show me again."

"Take my right hand in your left and place your right around my waist. Not so stiff. Becky is not a disease. Dancing with her won't poison you. Stop gritting your teeth."

"My teeth aren't the problem. It's my feet that are fixing to wander off and worry me."

"All right." Aunt Matty sighed. "While I step aside and watch, try it again with the chair."

"Okay."

Holding a kitchen chair in my arms, one that Papa had made, I whirled a turn or two, tripping only seven or eight times per step.

"Rob," said Aunt Matty, "you don't have to lift up your legs so high, like you're jumping a furrow. Slide your feet. Step, glide, step . . . the way I showed you. That's some better. But do try not to work your left arm up and down. You're dancing, not pumping water. And stop looking at your feet. Pretend you're on a dance floor. Not dodging pasture manure."

"Is that all?" I quit. "Anything else?"

"Smile," said our dancing expert. "With a handsome grin on your face, Miss Becky Lee Tate won't be able to wink at another thing. In your arms, she'll be floating on a star."

I smiled at the chair.

"Slide, slide," said Aunt Matty. "Step, glide, step. No! You're dragging a shoe. You and Becky won't be waltzing so rapid that you'll need to brake. It isn't downhill, and you're not a runaway wagon."

"Step, glide, step," I whispered to the chair. "Gee, I hope I'll be able to follow her."

"She'll be following you," Aunt Matty corrected. "You don't follow her. A girl isn't a plow." I tried again. "Smoother. Don't hustle it. You're not in a footrace. Keep time to the music."

"There isn't any."

"Perhaps," said Aunt Matty, "we ought to sing."

That's when Aunt Carrie busted out into *Onward Christian Soldiers*, until Aunt Matty suggested something other than a hymn and crooned up one of her favorites:

> *Oh . . . it's . . .*
> *Three o'clock in the morning.*
> *We danced the whole night through.*
> *Three o'clock in the morning.*
> *Just one more waltz with you.*

It wasn't easy to pick which was worse, my dancing or Aunt Matty's wavering soprano. As I practiced, I prayed my chair would feel like Becky Lee, tried not to look down to avoid a cow flop, and turned up my toes whenever I planted a heel. Also making certain that I kept Mr. Tanner's good church shoes, at all times, at least seven feet apart.

My legs straddled wider and wider, and then . . . I heard a nag of a noise.

Rip-p-p-p-p.

It sounded like my trouser seat, or rather, Will's. Holding my ladder-back partner by one hand, I made an exploratory search with the other, feeling, finding, and almost fainting. I could touch my underwear.

Mama inspected me.

OOOGA.

It was a Ford car horn.

"They're here," I said weakly.

"Hurry," said Mama to Carrie, "and fetch me a needle and black thread. Rob," she snapped at me, "sprawl yourself to my lap, face down, and don't twitch a hair."

"Yes'm." I stretched across Mama's knees.

"Let go of the chair," she said.

As I dropped my pine partner to the floor, Aunt Carrie returned at full gallop. Mama started to sew.

OOOGA. OOOOOGA.

"If anyone comes to the door," I pleaded, "please don't answer it. Just say there's nobody to home. Or that I broke both my legs."

While my mother sewed, Aunt Matty peeked out our only kitchen window, I sweated, and Aunt Carrie gave another go at *Onward Christian Soldiers*. On the floor, my chair became a sad, motionless wallflower.

"Here she comes!" Aunt Matty trilled. "Your sweetheart's coming toward the door."

"She is *not* my sweetheart," I protested, wishing, sort of, that she was. Then I heard her voice. And my name.

"Rob?"

KNOCK. KNOCK.

"Tell her I died," I whispered. "Say I got a rash all over me. No. Make it boils."

KNOCK.

"Hurry," said Becky, "or we might be so late that we'll miss parading in the Grand March."

Grand March? Well, at least I'd had a chance to rehearse *Onward Christian Soldiers*. If it was any other tune, I'd have to step-glide-trip-it all the way to first base. Or a dugout.

KNOCK. KNOCK. KNOCK.

"All done, Rob," said Mama.

Leaping up, hoping the thread would hold, I opened the door . . . to behold the prettiest princess in Learning, Vermont, in a pinky-white dress and a blue sash the color of my (Will Henry's) suit. Four women were all gushering at once while Mr. Tate beeped the horn. Grabbing my trembling hand, Becky hauled me toward the car, nearly dislocating my shoulder.

I tried to thank everyone.

Heading to the Grange Hall, I couldn't help worrying about the suit, my rip, and ballroom limitations.

Yet I didn't have to.

Sitting close beside me in the Ford sedan's roomy backseat (as her father was grinding the gears), Becky Lee squeezed my hand and smiled. Just for me. It made me feel taller than the King of England.

Miss Becky Lee Tate could certain turn a fellow grateful that he wouldn't be dancing a chair.

Chapter

5

June first arrived, a Saturday.

After breakfast, Mama and I spilled our teapot money on the kitchen table. Then counted it. We'd put by more than the twelve dollars that I'd carry to town.

The bills were all wrinkled up, so Mama heated an iron on the stove and pressed each one flat and tidy.

"Now don't lose it," Mama said.

Answering not a word, I stared at her real steady, to let her know I'd be toting our farm mortgage payment direct to the Learning Bank. Next to that, little mattered. The five acres would eventual become Peck property. Free and clear in four years. All ours.

Weeks ago, two days before he died, my father

had walked a May trip to Learning, to the bank. This would mark my first time.

It was a mile walk. But, seeing as I left our place after seven o'clock, and chores, I made Learning a minute or so before eight. In fact, I had to tarry outside before the bank opened its doors. I was the first person inside. As a lady approached, I took off my hat. Saying nothing, she eyed me and my clothes as though I'd come to rob the place. Before she could arrest me, I told her my business.

"My name is Robert Peck. You folks hold a mortgage on our farm. But we settle up proper. That's why I come. To pay."

"You're just a boy."

Touching my shirt pocket where the money hid, I said, "Please let me see the person who takes a mortgage payment. I got cash."

"Most people pay by check."

"I don't have one. All I brung is dollars."

"This way," she said coldly. "The cashier and the mortgage manager aren't here today, so I guess it will be all right if you deal with one of the bank's officers. The president is in. Come this way."

As she turned, I followed, chasing her along a row of doors with names on them in brass. At the end of the hall, she stopped to knock on the largest door.

"Yes?" a voice answered.

"Sorry to disturb you. There's a . . . a someone here to settle a mortgage payment." She asked me, "What was your name again?"

"Robert Peck."

"His name is Peck," she said to the door. "Something about a farm. He doesn't have a check."

The male voice said, "Henshaw handles that."

"Mr. Henshaw isn't in. Neither is Mr. Blake." She paused. "He's a boy, with cash. And Mr. Giblin isn't in yet. There's really no one else authorized to . . ."

"Very well. Show him in."

Opening the heavy wooden door, the lady turned to me. "You may enter." Closing the door behind me, she left, her shoes clicking down the hardwood hall.

As I walked in, hat in hand, the man's office was poorly lit. It smelled musty. Sort of like old clothes.

Before me, a gentleman in a dark suit sat with his back to me and to his boxy brown desk. He appeared to be sorting some papers on the windowsill. The bank president took his time before wheeling his high-backed chair around to face me. And what a surprise.

He was Mr. Haskell Gamp.

Seeing him made me drop my hat. And I didn't know whether to fetch it or run. My feet felt glued to his carpet.

"Morning," he said, with little appreciation of a new day.

I nodded.

There didn't seem to be any reason to tell him that only a few days ago, I'd been working at Mr. Tanner's when he'd arrived there, in a sorry state, with his mare. Well, I'd willing forget if he would. His face was granite. Perhaps, because I'd combed my hair (a rare ritual) this morning, he'd failed to recognize me.

"My name's Gamp. How may I serve you?"

Although respectful, his tone hinted that he probable had a pile of important matters to care for, and that I'd sprouted into his day as welcome as a weed in a flower bed. Behind his glasses, his eyes noticed my muddy boots as if concerned for his rug. He didn't stand or offer me a chair.

"We work a farm, sir," I said. "Uproad. My father always come to town to pay up, once a month. He's dead. So now it'll be my duty."

With only one word, Mr. Gamp slid open a desk drawer, his fingers walking along a stack of cream-colored folders. "Name?"

"Peck."

As I waited, he closed the drawer, opening another. "Ah," he said, "here it is, under the small accounts. But you aren't Haven Peck."

"No, sir. Mr. Haven Peck was my father. He died recent."

"I see. Regretful." He paused for a thinking. "And you, I now suppose, are here to make only partial payment and beg an extension. You can't afford to meet the full obligation. Is that it?"

I shook my head. "No, sir. I come to pay in full."

"You owe the bank . . . twelve dollars."

"Yes, sir."

Pulling the twelve ironed bills from my pocket, I showed Mr. Gamp the money, imagining that it meant little to him. It meant a lot to us.

"Now," he said, "seeing that your departed father is no longer, how do you expect to scrape up your monthly payment? Or, if you default, do you anticipate our bank to carry you?"

"We'll pay regular."

"On time? Every month for four years?"

"Yes, sir. On time, and in full."

"Tell me your age."

"Thirteen."

Checking the file, Mr. Gamp's face seemed to freeze. "These," he said, "are tight times. Several farms have been forced into insolvency. That means penniless. Broke. And no bank can risk capital on doubt."

Stepping forward, I placed our twelve dollar bills on the edge of his desk. "Sir, it's all there. Every cent. And next month I'll be here again with another twelve. We'll pay our due."

"Who else resides on your property?"

"My mother and my aunt."

"They're both women." His clean, unworked hand counted our cash. "A lot of these uproader farms go under. Bad risks for a bank. That goes double with no adult male to work the land." Looking up, his eyes narrowed behind rimless glasses. "Your ox died."

His remark startled me.

"How did you know that, sir?"

"An alert bank keeps tabs on almost everyone in town, especially families with mortgages. It's my position to predict disaster before it occurs, thereby

— 46 —

saving the bank money by avoiding any defaulted payment. Be my guess that, with no ox, you'll be unable to glean much profit from the place. Little or none."

Opening another drawer, Mr. Gamp produced a map, unfolded it, then studied it for over a minute.

"Here it is." His fingertip tapped the paper. "Peck, five acres. It's hilly property. Class D. You're located, however, south of some Class AB, the Tanner parcel. Is that so?"

"Yes, sir." I held my breath.

"When he was alive, what else besides farming did your father do? Mill work?"

"No, sir. Papa killed hogs for Mr. Clay Sander."

"I see. But now, without such income, your family could become destitute and financially delinquent. In debt. Other than house and real property, that means land, what other assets can you claim? What's your livestock?"

"Chickens, about twenty or so. And a cow." I didn't bother to mention that Daisy was dry.

"Any saleable machinery?"

"No, sir. We run our farm mostly by hand."

Refolding the map, Mr. Gamp tucked it back inside his desk.

"Seems to me, you Peck people ought to consider selling out."

"But it's our home. Sir, we live there. I never lived a day nowhere else, and don't aim."

Mr. Gamp snorted. "The country's in hard times. A possible depression. If the bank decides to propose an offer for your place, my advice to you, sonny, is to consider it serious. Grab whatever you can get."

I stood straighter.

"Our farm is not for sale." I took a breath. "We Pecks aren't in debt. Not a penny."

"No, not yet." Mr. Gamp smirked. "But a hundred forty-four dollars a year might climb beyond your ability to meet. Four years at that figure of obligation adds up to over five hundred." His mouth smiled, but not his eyes. "Plus taxes."

My body became wet. "Taxes?"

"Youngster, your annual property tax falls due in September, like everyone else's. In the past twenty years, plenty of farms fell into foreclosure and forfeit. Tax failure. Current rate is seven per acre. So, come the first dawn of September, you'll owe the township thirty-five dollars. Or else."

I wanted to walk out of Mr. Gamp's office and then run home, to stand on my own property, not his, and breathe my own sweet air. Yet I couldn't seem to budge a boot.

The banker stared at me. As his eyebrows raised, he said, "Say, I've seen you somewhere before. That face of yours looks familiar. Where was it?"

There was no use in lying.

"At Mr. Tanner's. About two weeks ago."

The lines in Mr. Gamp's face deepened. "So," he said slowly, "now I do recall. I was ill that day. Fighting a flu. A gentleman has a right to spirits for medicinal purpose."

"Ben Tanner took thirty-seven stitches. And he didn't have a right to even one."

"Here," said Mr. Gamp, suddenly standing to hand me a pen. "Put your X mark to this paper," he snapped, "where it says June." He pointed to the line with his finger.

Glancing down, I saw where Papa, unable to sign his name, had crossed so many marks, for so long a time. I wanted to touch and bless every X he'd made, something that a banker such as Mr. Gamp wouldn't understand.

Instead of X, I wrote Robert Newton Peck on the line. Papa would have been proud.

Snatching the pen from my fingers, Mr. Gamp said, "You are a rude and uppity boy. You don't know your place. However, business is business, and the bank will credit your account with the customary twelve dollars. Good day."

"Thank you, sir. You'll see me again in July, and August, and every single month until the farm is all ours."

Picking up my hat, I left smiling.

Chapter

6

School let out.

Becky Tate had coaxed me to attend with more devotion, so I wasn't worried much about failure. But I didn't want to flunk English or hurt Miss Malcolm. Now there were more mature matters on my mind. Taxes due in September plus monthly bank payments might threaten the deed to our farm. The death of Solomon was one problem. A second one was now walking behind me.

As I led Daisy, our milk cow, by a rope and halter, I headed over the ridge toward Mr. Tanner's. Ben and I had talked it over and shook on a bargain. I'd work three days for free if his bull would freshen Daisy.

Arriving, I was about to tie the loose end of her rope to a fence post when Ben hobbled out of the house to greet me.

"Beowolf's ready for her," Ben said, eyeing my old cow. "The question is, will she be ready for him?"

"He'd always do her before."

"True. But a bull has preferences. The younger the heifer, the more eager he is to mount and mate, providing her scent is strong enough to bait him."

Ben's sober face warned me.

Walking beside him, I noticed a gimpy gait, as though every step cut into him.

"Are you mending, Ben?"

"Gradual, a day at a time. You can't kill a Vermonter. We just wear out like a pair of pants. Last evening, Bess pulled out my stitches. Smarted near as bad as going in."

"Mr. Gamp did wrong to you."

"Indeed so. But Mr. Gamp regretted it and stopped by here the other day to apologize." Ben smiled. "In fact, he brought me a cheese."

"He still made a mistake with his mare."

"Robert, we all make a misstep now and again. Every man has a weakness. I'd be flimsy if I held a grudge against Haskell Gamp." Ben sighed. "Forgiveness heals a hurt better than iodine or thread."

The kindly way he said it made me respect Benjamin Franklin Tanner all the more.

Leading Daisy, we rounded a corner of Ben's big cow barn. There he stood. Beowolf, a black-and-white Holstein bull. A giant. Ben looked at him with pride, then at me, and bent a slow grin.

"I'll never forget that Sunday afternoon," he said. "You were maybe half as high as now. You stood here with your folks, and so did our preacher and his wife, Reverend Hazeltine and Mrs."

"I don't recall."

Ben laughed. "Well, I do. Bess mentioned it recent. We were all standing right here, admiring Beowolf, when he took a big breath and roared one mighty bellow. Mrs. Hazeltine said . . . *My, what a pair of lungs.* And you, young Robert, pointed at his hinder, and said . . . *Those aren't lungs. Them are his* . . . and your ma muffled your mouth not a second too soon."

I felt my face redden. "Did I say that? If so, I certain am sorry."

Ben rested a hand on my shoulder. "No need. There's nothing evil or dirty about nature. What made it all so amusing was the fact that your father attempted a smile. And that was a feat he'd perform about once a decade." Ben sighed. "I miss Haven. Always a good steady neighbor. All salt and no pepper."

I couldn't say anything. When my father died,

it was as though God had ripped the sun from out of my sky. I become a lantern with no light.

"Bess and I were never blessed with children. Now that we're aging into ancient, Rob, we sort of think of you as ours. Not that I'd ever try to replace your father. No one could replace Haven Peck. But both Bess and I feel close to you and your folks."

"We feel likewise."

Daisy muttered a soft *moo*.

"Smell him, Daisy," Ben said to our cow. "Help yourself to a whiff of my bull."

"You smell too, Beowolf," I said hopefully. "It's spring."

Walking behind her, Ben lifted Daisy's tail, smelled her, and touched her. Then he shook his head.

"Little chance," he told me. "No heat. She's like winter. Cold enough to freeze the balls off a pool table. It's June, boy. But for that cow of yourn, it's the dark of December."

Beowolf didn't even glance our way.

Ben pointed at his bull. "That old Romeo knows more than you, me, and Daisy all put together. We got a pair of disinterested parties, Rob. My advice to you is to end her." Kneeling, he felt her udder. "Empty as a Monday church."

"What'll I do with her?"

"For your heart's sake, turn her out into your meadow for a spell. Let her graze, fatten, and enjoy the summer. But by autumn, best you not waste even one wisp of hay to board her all winter. You can't afford that. Daisy will never again lactate. But don't delay, Robert. Best you sell her while she's still alive. If she dies, you'll have naught."

"Sell her? Who'd buy a dry cow? What would she be good for?"

"Dog meat."

I closed my eyes. "No. I can't."

"Wake up, boy. Yes, you can because you'll have to do just that, and no other. There isn't a choosing. Only an end. Daisy's had a good life among you Pecks. Now, young man, best be growed-up enough to face what's so. These are hard truths they don't teach you in school. Like it or no, it's what I do with my old cows. You'll get five dollars for her and no more."

"How would I go about selling her?"

"Go to Clay Sander. Your pa killed his hogs for many a year. Clay'll handle it."

While I was leading Daisy back to our place, I stopped on the ridge that separated the Tanner property from ours. From up here, I could breathe air so fresh that I could almost drink it, and look down to our house and barn. We had Solomon no longer. And soon, there'd be no Daisy.

My hand touched her warm body on the right side, where my father would so often rest his head while milking her.

"Daisy," I said, "why do we always have to lose so many animals and people that belong to us? Why?"

Sometime I'd have to bury both Mama and Aunt Carrie. One by one. Even though it was a warm June morning, the thought of their going turned me chilly. Ben Tanner had told me, less than a hour ago, that I would have to get growed-up. That meant a Shaker accepting of both life and death. There was no way to part one from the other.

"Dog meat." I said it aloud, so I would toughen enough to swallow what's real. The words knifed into me. Standing there, looking down at our little farm, I wanted to be a boy again, with all around me that I knew and felt a part of. And no banking.

Perhaps I'd been too rude to Mr. Gamp.

The urge to apologize had simmered inside me since that Saturday morning at the bank. Neither my father nor my mother would have spoke what I told him. My feelings were right, yet my reason was wrong.

Ben Tanner, in his silent way, had forgiven Mr. Gamp's error. And if Ben could do it, tore apart, then so could Rob Peck. Made little sense to carry a hate. The load of it was burdensome. Too heavy to haul.

Above me, the sun had been behind a cloud, but it sudden shined on me, warming the all of my person.

"Daisy," I said, "let's go home."

Together, we walked down off the ridge to our place, to where we belonged. Peck land. Bending, I scooped up a clod of earth. In my hand it felt fresh and fertile, a woman awaiting seed.

The day was still young. So I turned Daisy out into our meadow and made for the barn, and the many bags of seed corn that had rested there all winter long.

Later, I was broadcasting. For years I'd watched Papa do it, walking our cornfield in May or early June with a sack of seed beneath his left armpit. He'd walk along steady and slow, at an even pace, never slowing, grabbing a handful of corn kernels. Then he'd hurl it in an arc before him, again and again, until his sack no longer bulged but sagged to empty. I felt proud to walk where he had walked. Following my father.

The seeding took all day. Farming by hand is

slow work. Yet with each hurling of my arm and scattering of seed, I felt renewed. Born again.

This wouldn't be table corn. It was silage. Field corn. With no Solomon and no Daisy, I could turn these two acres, that Solomon and I had plowed, into a money crop. For taxes. A pity that neither Solomon or Daisy would winter on what I now was sowing. Yet, in a way, I was working in their honor; they prospered on our land.

I broadcasted my final bag.

Sun would shine, and the wind and rain would help bury every seed. Easier than covering it with a hoe. Nature would be tucking my corn kernels into bed like wee children. All snug.

Deep in the earth, a seed would begin to sprout and prosper. I'd broadcast. God, the Giver, would do the rest. Standing alone on a fresh-seeded field, the flow of farming was uplifting me. Up through my bare feet. An old Shaker saying crossed my mind, something Papa had told me: "Gratefulness is the highest note in the hymn of prayer."

Years ago, when I'd attended a local one-room schoolhouse during my early years of education, Miss Kelly had said likewise.

"Teachers," she said, "are like farmers. We are in charge of the green and the growing. Every morning, a farmer goes to his garden. Yet, in a way, a teacher is luckier because my garden comes to me."

For some reason, I kept on standing out in the field of fresh-seeded corn. Alone with the Almighty. The pair of us. And I couldn't have been granted a more worthy partner. Right then, I decided that I'd never beg the Lord to carry me through. But only that He would afford me the back to do it.

"Hear me," I told the sunshine. "I'm no longer a boy. You seen fit to promote me to manhood, so that's what I'll be. A man."

Looking at my skinny arms, I began to wonder if'n I'd muster up the might. No way I'd ever share my doubts with Mama or Aunt Carrie. To them, I'd be a rock. Their hope. Six months before my father died, he'd prepared me . . . "It's got to be you, Rob. There's nobody else. It has just got to be you."

I blinked at a blue sky.

Chapter

7

Time for haying.

Wading through less than two acres of hay, I could feel the green shafts of timothy swishing against my bare feet and ankles, and smell the fresh-cut clover.

The hay was ripe, ready to mow. Light green, almost a gray. Below, low to ground, the thicker clumps of clover seemed Sunday dressed with flowering balls of lavender and white.

"A money crop," I said, "to keep our farm."

My shirt was wet with work. Salty sweat was stinging my eyes, so I rested my tall two-handed scythe to rag my face. Seeds stuck to me. Pulling a gray whetstone from a back pocket, I turned the scythe upside down to click a fresh edge on a long curving blade. The sound carried. Another reaper, beyond sight, answered me with his stone, as if to brag that he was working as hard. It was a sort of summer music, a rhythm, to hear a whetstone strum a scythe.

I continued to mow, inching forward step by step with every sweeping swing. It felt manly to earn money. Ben, because of his injury, wouldn't be haying as much. He usual offered seven dollars a ton. But that was delivered to his hay barn. Now, without Solomon, I'd have to chop my price to five dollars a ton because his man George would have to come with their oxen and wagon. By then, I'd have it all down, tumbled into straight windrows, and then piled as soon as dry.

As I worked, I remembered last summer. My father was haying beside me. He'd nearly stomped on a nest when a swallow fluttered up to scold. Together, we knelt to locate her four young birdlets, barely hatched. Fuzz instead of feathers. Papa halted his work, fetched a beanpole, and marked her nesting place, to spare the little miracle that happened in his hay.

"Papa."

The echo of his name wafted away, and I stood alone in our hayfield with the cut of a memory.

As the June sun was hot in a cloudless sky, the mowed hay behind me was drying. Mama and Aunt Carrie come out with pitchforks to tumble it. In the kitchen, they talked. But here they spoke little. Hour after hour, they worked silent as men.

At supper that evening, I noticed the tired on their faces. Neither one complained. Perhaps their backs told them that I ached as did they. When we bowed our heads for a Shaker blessing, I saw their hardened hands clenched in grace; they asked for so little, and yet they'd given so much.

"Bless our food," Mama whispered with her eyes closed, "and us for Thy service, to Kingdom Hall. Amen."

"Amen," said Carrie and I.

Supper was beans, boiled eggs, and turnip greens, and milk, given to me by Mrs. Tanner. Soon I'd wring a chicken's neck, and we'd feast for fair. We ate no beef, no pork, and no mutton.

"Tomorrow," I told them as I ate, "I'm taking Daisy away. There's no other answer. Ben says she'll never again freshen, and he's raised more cows than I have."

Mama and Carrie stopped eating.

"Please," I said, "don't poke me with questions. It's for the farm's good. For us."

Inside, my mind harped on the threat of our September taxes. My ears still rang with Mr. Gamp's warning of the money we'd owe.

"Robert," said Mama, "you'll act right. We trust. So don't you fret a mite. Do what needs."

Aunt Carrie nodded.

Looking at both of them, I said, "You ladies are Vermont granite. There's not a farm in the county that can boast of two women, or two men, the such of you."

Mama smiled faintly.

"Yoke us," she said, "and we'll pull."

After supper, while Mama and Aunt Carrie were ragging the kitchen, I went outside. As it was still light, I walked to the hayfield to sweep another swath. In my hands, the scythe seemed heavier, and its edge duller. Hay almost refused to fall. But I reaped until after sundown before returning my cutter to the toolshed, where I wiped clean its blade.

As I passed the henhouse, the chickens were either asleep or in prayer. Nary a peep.

Standing at the meadow fence, I allowed my chin to rest on the butt of a post. How many tons of hay, I wondered, would we glean? Not enough for September. Thirty-five dollars was a fortune. Was Mr. Gamp right? Maybe selling the farm was sound.

"No," I said, lifting my head.

Daisy must have been listening. Because I saw

her strolling toward me in the moonlight, walking very slowly across the stubby pasture grass.

"Howdy, old girl. I know. You miss old Solomon."

Do cows think? Standing there, leaning on the fence, I figured Daisy realized that something in her life was different. My twice-a-day visits had ended. More than missing her milk, I missed milking her, feeling all of her hay-burned warmth. And I was hoping that Daisy missed me as much.

It had been a long day.

My eyes felt already asleep. Saying a good-night to Daisy, I trudged up to the gentle knoll to our house. A lantern yellowed our kitchen window. By itself. Mama and Aunt Carrie had crept into bed.

Just as I was inhaling to blow out the kitchen light, Sarah, our cat, came from behind the stove, tail high, to rub against my leg. Bending, I petted her. Then, picking her up into my arms, I held her purring against my face. Miss Sarah was warm and soft. Yet she felt older to me, and thinner.

"Miss Sarah," I told her, "we still have you, little pet. You're older than I am."

For some reason, I lay down on the hard boards of our kitchen floor, allowing Sarah to lie on my chest. Paws primly together, she blinked at me, closing her eyes with the complete contentment that belongs only to a cat.

"Sarah," I whispered to her. "Miss Sarah."

Stroking her, I thought of Daisy, alone out in our meadow night, perhaps longing for Solomon's company. Animals feel. This I knew. They touch and are touched. Words weren't no more than extra weight. Friendship took no talking.

Nearly asleep, I tried not to think about tomorrow, or Daisy, or Mr. Clay Sander. As Miss Sarah hopped off my chest, my eyes opened, so I made myself undress, wash, and tumble into bed.

I slept on a tick. A muslin sack, tan as an eggshell, stuffed with dried corn shucks. It allowed a sleeper to smell last summer's corn all winter, a cozy lullaby for a January night. Curling up on a tick made a rustle of rest. Beneath me, the cradling crackle of tick stuffing whispered me a bedtime story softer than a twilight kiss.

That's all I remembered.

Early next morning, I led Daisy to Clay Sander's butchery to cut a business deal with him. As I collected the five dollars in cash, my hand was trembling. I hated the feel of it. Lucky for me, the words *dog meat* never got spoken. Had I heard them, I might've turned tail and run away, taking

Daisy with me. Or worse, just leaving her behind.

This, however, was no time to be a coward. Instead, I stayed with her for over an hour because I wouldn't allow her final moments of life to be among strangers who didn't care or even know her name.

A man came and tagged her, twisting a wire around the base of her ear. He looked at me.

"Your cow?"

"Yes, sir."

"Maybe you'd best leave, boy. Because I don't guess you'll want to watch. It ain't pleasant."

"I'll stay."

With a shrug, the man gently punched my shoulder, then left me alone with Daisy. The stink of the place was strong. A death smell. With my arms around her warm neck, I hugged her for a final time, saying "Daisy" to her. She wasn't easy to hold. Her head fought the rope.

The man returned with another man. Both of them were wearing leather aprons.

"Bring her," one of them said.

I led her inside, onto a concrete walkway, and they vised her head into a stanchion below a platform. A man climbed the short ladder to stand above her and picked up a sledgehammer.

Daisy kicked, but there was no escape.

As I leaned forward to touch my face to hers, I heard "Back away, boy."

I obeyed. But I remained near, eyes closed tight, until I heard that dull horrid sound of a sledge bashing her skull under the little curlycue between her eyes. I heard her fall. She was dead.

Only when the men were fastening a heavy chain to one of her hind legs did I leave her. Behind me, the rattle of the chain in its conveyor track grew fainter as I began my lonely walk.

To honor her, on the way home I kept repeating Daisy's name, hoping somehow, and somewhere green, she was with Solomon.

Chapter

8

Good news.

I passed English. Only because Becky Lee Tate had, for some odd reason, enjoyed the dance at the Grange Hall, and had coached me. Lucky for me, on Miss Malcolm's final English test there was only one question on *As You Like It*.

Who wrote it? And I could answer that.

My really pleasant surprise arrived one morning when I was standing between two short rows of dill, and along come Miss Malcolm on the dirt road.

"Robert," she cried, grunting her weight out of her junky two-seater car, "you rascal, you never came to school to pick up your year-end report card. Even though your attendance record needs improving."

There I stood, smeared with manure dust, as I'd been pushing wheelbarrows of it to our vegetable garden.

"Did I pass?"

She smiled at me. "Somehow. Even though you and Becky Tate wrote a few mysteriously similar answers."

When she handed me the card, I first wiped my hands on my pants. "Thanks. Thank you a lot, Miss Malcolm."

"You're quite welcome." She paused. "At school, we teachers are aware of your father's death, and that now you're working the farm. We salute your resolution."

"Well, I'm giving it a go."

"Please don't drop out of school. We need you there. You need us. The poem that you handed in . . ."

"No good?"

"On the contrary. I thought it outstanding. I'm going to copy it and save it at home, in a very special box where I keep important papers. I can't remember all of it, only the last four lines . . .

A farmer's heart is rabbit soft.
And farmer eyes are blue.

But farmers' eyes are eagle fierce,
To look a man right through."

"The farmer was my father."

"Yes, I guessed as much." Miss Malcolm's face turned serious. "Why, when you have talent, did you waste your school time, last October, playing that prank on the shop teacher, Mr. Orr?"

"I'm sorry."

"You ought to be." Miss Malcolm stamped her foot. "You and that Jacob Henry deserved a scolding or a spanking, and possibly both. The pair of you are more slippery than wet seeds."

Looking down at my dirty bare feet, I asked, "How did you find out *we* did it?"

"Word," said Miss Malcolm, "gets around. Wherever did you boys get that," she paused, ". . . that *publication*?"

"From out of the trash can. You know, in the alley behind Rocco's Barbershop."

"I hardly spend much time there. Nor do I ever review Mr. Rocco's reading material."

"Sorry, I didn't mean it that way."

Miss Malcolm pointed a finger at me. "Well, a trash can is exactly where those . . . those shocking girlie-girlie magazines belong. Bad enough that you and Jacob even bothered to flip through them.

But no, you two sneaked one to school. Then, on that downpour of a rainy day, you hid it inside old Mr. Orr's umbrella."

"What happened wasn't really part of the joke."

"I know what happened! I was there, standing with Miss Johnson and Miss Wickersham in front of the school waiting for the rain to stop. And poor Mr. Orr opened his umbrella. Out that girlie book tumbled, to reveal that . . . that *photography*."

"Yes'm."

"Miss Wickersham is very straitlaced. And I thought she would either scream or faint. She was gasping."

"Yes'm. I'm sorry. We didn't count on blushing any of the lady teachers. Honest. Only Mr. Orr." I scratched myself. "How did he know who did it?"

"Mr. Orr may be aging and deaf, but I assure you, he didn't need Sherlock Holmes to finger the culprits, because earlier, he had threatened to thrash both you and the Henry boy, and you know why."

I nodded. "Oh, that was sort of in fun. During woodshop, we nailed his glove, from the inside, to the plank of his workbench."

"He caught you doing it?"

"Not exactly. But when Pop Orr . . . excuse me,

I meant Mr. Orr . . . couldn't pick up his glove and cussed, the other boys all laughed and looked at Jacob and me."

Right then, I was praying that Miss Malcolm wouldn't blame either Jacob or me for what three of the high school guys did. Late one night, they painted a sign, and then hung it over Pop Orr's front door. The letters were bright red.

ORR HOUSE

Miss Malcolm stared at me. "I'd dread to imagine what goes on inside that brain of yours."

"Thoughts I don't write down."

"Robert, perhaps you *should* write them."

"Yes'm."

Entering her beat-up car, Miss Malcolm looked at me from behind the wheel. "Write another poem." She winked at me with a nod of her gray hair.

"I will, Miss Malcolm."

"Promise?"

"Yes'm."

"Oh, one more thing. Learn to dance."

I made a face. "How did you know I couldn't? I get it. You must've served at the Grange Hall that evening, as one of the Percherons."

"I believe," said my teacher, "the correct word is *chaperone*. A Percheron is a big heavy horse with hairy ankles."

I covered my mouth and my giggle.

"Robert, not one word." She paused. "You never saw me at the Grange; you were too entranced with Miss Tate. By the way, I met her earlier. She's going to come out here this afternoon."

"Why?"

"Because, according to Becky, a lot of the other kids are vacationing. Having fun. She knows you've been working seven days a week. So she's taking you somewhere."

I gulped. "Where?"

"On a picnic. I suggest you bathe."

Miss Malcolm drove away. But I couldn't make a move. My toes seemed to be rooted into mud, and manure. One inhale told me that I'd best search for soap. At the outdoor pump, I stripped and lathered and washed, rubbing myself to raw. Then I splashed on some of Aunt Carrie's lilac water and dabbed a lick of Papa's pomade to my hair. I was wearing only a towel when Mama spied me, come close, and her nose took a breath of my flowery scent.

"My," she said, "I didn't aware it was Saturday night."

"Becky's coming."

"Who said?"

"Miss Malcolm. I passed English and all else. She stopped by to warn me about Becky Lee."

"To warn you? Becky's hardly a storm."

"At least for this time," I told Mama, "I won't have to do dancing. Does my hair look respectful? It won't part."

"Here," she said, taking the comb. "Begin by slicking it all forward. Like this. Now we'll divide it right down the middle." She groomed me. "There."

"Do I look all right?"

"Sharp as a new pin. And handsome. People might mistake you for that knight gentleman you were telling me about. You know, in that book."

"Ivanhoe."

"I believe that's his name."

"Do I really look as good as he does?"

Wiping her hands on her apron, Mama said, "Seeing as I haven't run into Mr. Ivanhoe lately, I couldn't say certain. But he couldn't scrub up any cleaner."

In the house, I pulled on a fresh shirt and pants. June was too sunny for shoes. Barefoot, I ran outside just in time to see a Ford motorcar out by the dirt road. It stopped. Out popped Becky Lee Tate, wearing a pretty white dress and toting a wicker basket. Mr. Tate waved and chugged off toward town.

"Howdy," I said, going to meet Becky as she was skipping my way.

"I'm taking you on a picnic, Rob."

"Hey, great."

"Where'll we go? Someplace private."

I knew a perfect spot. Down along the crickbed there was a grassy place under a stand of slender white birch trees. Holding the basket with one hand, and Becky's hand with the other, I took her there.

The crick gurgled shallow over a quilt of smooth pebbles all shades of fawn, and I knew the cool water here tasted clear and sweet. Cracking open the basket, Becky pulled out a red-and-white checkerboard cloth and then covered it with cold chicken, apples, egg sandwiches, pickles, a slab of cheese, pie, and wedges of raw cabbage. Plus two chocolate cupcakes. She'd even squeezed lemonade.

While I ate, Becky sat there looking more delicious than dessert and listened to me chew. She only ate part of a sandwich. That left three and a half for me. Add to that seven pickles and both apples. Becky Lee sipped lemonade as I licked chocolate off my fingers.

"Try a napkin," she said, tossing one at me.

"No need. Be a shame to waste chocolate on cloth."

"Please use it. I want your mouth tidy."

I kept licking. "How come?"

"Because today is a very special day." Becky smiled softly. "It's my birthday. I'm thirteen."

"Well," I said, "happy birthday, Becky." I grinned at her. "Maybe I ought to give you thirteen spanks."

"Don't you dare." She lowered her eyes. "Besides, that is not the kind of present that I wanted from you. You'll have to guess."

I stopped licking the cupcake chocolate. "Golly, I didn't suspect it was your birthday. I don't have a present."

"Yes, you do. It can be the gift you forgot to give me when the dance was over. I bet I was the only girl who went home empty."

Was she talking about food? Perhaps so, because after the dance ended, some of the kids skipped across the road to the diner for ice cream. But I had no money for frills. I was hoping Becky would realize, and understand.

Maybe she did. Yet, for certain, I really didn't begin to understand *her*. Because now she was leaning closer to me with her eyes shut. It didn't appear as though she was still waiting for ice cream.

"Rob," she whispered, "please kiss me. And do it sudden quick, before you lose your nerve."

Hearing her say it pleased me like pudding. So I bent close and kissed her on the cheek, and did it softer than a Sunday prayer. I had to dodge her mouth to do it.

"Now," she said, "do it right. I want you to kiss me that same way, but not on my cheek. Kiss my lips."

I did. And she kissed me back. We sort of took turns at kissing each other. Believe me, not the best chocolate cupcake in the world tasted half as savory as Becky Lee Tate.

Becky looked in my eyes, smiling, and then whispered to me like a summer song.

"As you like it."

Chapter

9

We made our July mortgage due. Yet in the Learning area, there wasn't a single farmer that had been blessed by July.

It didn't rain. Overhead, the heavens clouded over, but the moisture seemed to pass by. At this rate, there'd be no second cutting of hay. My corn was up, but it refused to make or stay green. Ben Tanner's corn looked near as puny.

I went to Ben's for advice.

Stooping, he touched the brown corn leaves. So did I. They felt parched and brittle. Ben's hand plucked one. As he stood, he fingered the leaf slowly and sadly.

"Dry," he said. "Dryer than a nun's bun. And there's naught we can do to help."

Mr. Tanner had planted far more acres than had

I. My loss would be nothing compared with his.

I hurried home, where our outside yard pump had already coughed out to dead dry. Mama and Carrie were in the kitchen dusting out canning jars for August. It could be a waste of work.

"We can save the crop," I said.

Mama looked surprised. "How?"

"If the three of us are willing to burden buckets of water up from the crick, we'll water by hand. We only got two corn acres."

Mama looked at her elder sister. "Can you help?"

With a set jaw, Aunt Carrie nodded. "If need be," she said. "Right now, with only a spoon of water, Lucy, I could charge Hell."

In our barn we grabbed three buckets. They were enough. From the crick, and uphill every step, I carried two buckets of water, while my mother and aunt shared one between them.

It took a whole bucket of water to soak one corn plant. That was the first trip. Again and again we returned to a low crick to refill our pails.

Above, the July sun was merciless; in no shade the heat was hitting us like a hammer. At the crick, I made Mama and Carrie remove their aprons (which they almost always wore) and I soaked them, then wrapped the wet aprons around their sweating, sunburnt heads. Their gray hair was already damp.

All day we worked. Three buckets at a trip. Even though I was lugging four times the weight they each carried, I felt hardy enough to hack it.

I made both of them rest under an elm while I returned to the barn for rags. The bucket handles were hurting our hands. And inside the house I found their two white bonnets. Rags helped. But not much.

Out yonder, on the dirt road, a car stopped. People got out to watch us. The car looked the fancy type. City folks. One of them pointed at us, as though we were fools. Another fetched out a camera and took our picture. We didn't pose, or smile and wave friendly. Instead, we kept on a-going in the heat, crossing and recrossing the awnless anvil under a hammering sun.

"They know what we're doing, Mama."

Wiping her face, my mother let out a huff. "Them tourist people don't know beans." She looked at me slow. "Or corn."

I wanted to shout, to tell them to move along on, knowing that it'd be a waste of work. Spent air.

Mama studied the sky. "No pity, Carrie. That old sun's got no soul. Not even for sinners like us."

"Let's keep going," I said, "and remember what Papa taught me about working a chore. A man don't quit at tired. He only quits at done."

"Lucy," said my aunt, "let's haul water."

We kept doing. How, I don't know, because my hands felt as though knuckles would rub earth. My arms stretched to eight foot long.

I'd lost count.

When we'd commenced, I'd begun to number our trips; uphill at full, and then returning to the crickbed empty. Now the late afternoon and evening had blended into endless effort. None of the three of us wanted to be the first to beg a halt.

"One more," I'd say again, and often. "Just one more carry, and maybe we'll call it a day."

Yet we refused to surrender. No drought could beat us down or dry. During usual times, our neighbors and friends and some other Shakers might have come to help us. But no. Because each of their properties had a thirst of its own.

The sun sank.

"We're done," I told them. "There's no moon, and we can't no longer see. Best we hang up our buckets until morning."

There was no argument.

Mama merely said, "Rob, whatever you deem right."

We ate a cold supper.

While we'd been working, hauling water, the kitchen stove had gone out. I didn't care a bit of a bother. Neither did they. We just sat at the table, grateful that the big black Acme American stove was cold, and ate. Cold beans and some stale bread topped with our last jar of blackberry jam from last season.

"Stars," said Mama. "We forgot blessing."

We bowed. My mother spoke in a frail voice. "There's others," she said quietly, "that don't sit to near fancy as this. Please bless 'em, Lord. Amen."

Never in my life had I felt so grateful.

Following supper, by a feeble lantern, I had to lift up Aunt Carrie and burden her to bed. She was olden, and, in my arms, not much more than a wore-out ragdoll. Returning to the kitchen, I saw Mama sitting at the table, eyes closed. Going to her, I wrapped both arms around her and realized my wealth.

"Robert," she said to me in a whisper, "are we going to make do?" She paused. "Please don't ask me for thinking. I'm an old shoe that's wore out to the stocking."

I couldn't say a word.

"Haven," my mother said, "come back."

Patting her shoulder, still damp from the labor, I said, "He's gone. But if'n he was here, he'd be rightful proud of you, and of Carrie."

"Do you figure we saved our corn?"

Pushing aside all my doubts, I told her, "Yes. We rescued it for today. Tomorrow, I just bet it'll rain. We'll listen up thunder. The skies will turn to pure purple, and all them little raindrops will shower our fields. Every inch. You wait and see, Mama. It's going to soak us enough to spook Noah."

She looked at me. "Please," she said, "go fetch The Book."

I did as she'd asked.

Upstairs, underneath the bed my parents had slept in, they kept a Bible box. In it, the most precious thing we owned. I brought The Book that my parents could never read but knew so well.

"Read," she said. "I ache to hear it. Please let it wash me clean, like the feet of His Twelve."

"Which part, Mama?"

"Genesis. But you're tired as I, so read me one rainy verse, and that shall sustain me until sleep."

Turning to the seventh chapter of Genesis, I read to my mother; verse twelve, the place she had spoken: "And the rain was upon the earth . . . forty days and forty nights."

I closed The Book.

"Good," she said. "I'm so thankful that you can read what's written, so long ago, and on this night so neighborly."

"Maybe," I said, "you ought to go upstairs."

"In a moment. For now, sit with me, Robert. You're my one surviving son. Charles and Edward were taken from us, buried in our little orchard among the four apple trees. Your sisters have departed to far places, with husbands and kinder of their own. Of my brood, all I have left is you, Robert. You are my last. Yet never let it be uttered that you be least."

Smiling, I said, "I'm certain the most used up."

"And I."

"Mama, we Pecks aren't the only family that got burnt by the dry spell. It hit everyone. Rich and poor alike. Mr. Tanner's corn is wilted near to dust."

My mother touched my hand. "I know. Many's the time I've climbed up that ridge to view the Tanner farm. All their fine barns and buildings. And stock. But I wouldn't trade for all of it."

It made me grin. "Mama, right about now I'd swap myself in for half a bag of potatoes."

"Being tired does that, son. Some days, you can't feel to be more than a empty bucket."

"We emptied them today."

Mama nodded. "Multitudes."

Her head sagged. Eyelids at half mast, as though the fire within her had blowed out. Grayed to ashes.

"Bedtime," I said to her.

"Indeed so."

"Upstairs I left a lantern burning, so you won't stumble around up yonder."

Mama stood. "When I snuff it, even before the light fails, I'll be dreaming."

"Dream good things."

"I will, son."

She refused my offer to help her up the stairs. One by each, my mother made it all the way. From the kitchen, I heard the rustle of her tick and knew she was safe abed. Nothing left to do except supper dishes. Those I washed in a breath. We'd saved enough pump water.

Before going to my tick, I went outdoors to whisper a good-night to the moon. Stars were out. The sky was a dark meadow of fireflies. It made me wonder if a certain girl was sleeping.

My Becky Lee.

Chapter

10

The first of August.

But because of the lack of rain, our little vegetable garden didn't fare. Beets were the size of peas. So I had to raid Mama's teapot in order to trade for beans, flour, carrots, onions, plus a sack of barley, and cornmeal. Even our laying hens seemed to go on strike. Every morning, I'd find fewer eggs in the henhouse. Two hens died. So did our rooster. Worse yet, we couldn't muster up our twelve dollars for the Learning Bank.

One morning, as I was hauling more buckets of crick water to our vegetable patch, I heard a motorcar. Squinting over at the road, I noticed one I hadn't seen before. It stopped. Two men, both wearing suits and ties, got out.

Staying close to the car, they looked at a map,

pointing to our burnt corn, the shabby hayfield stubble, and then toward our house and barn.

Pretending not to be interested, I reset a pole for bean vines to climb. Instead of being curly soft and searching, the vine looked brown. In my fingers it felt hard and dying. I heard voices. Moving closer and out of sight, I walked near enough to overhear the two men.

One was the banker, Mr. Haskell Gamp.

"It'll go," he was saying.

"You sure, Haskell? Because if'n no, then I'm mere frittering my time up here."

Mr. Gamp nodded. "Believe me, Mayland, this here piece of property will go for taxes."

"No equity."

"Some. More'n one would think. Until recent, the farmer was a man named Peck. Haven Peck died last May." He pointed at our house. "In that shack there's a surviving widow, a schoolboy, and one other . . . an old spinster aunt."

Turning to Mr. Gamp, the other man pointed a finger at his vest and said, "I'm not about to court trouble. Bad publicity."

"Won't be any."

"What do you think this place is worth?"

Removing his hat, Mr. Gamp blotted his brow with a white handkerchief, returned it to his pocket, and said, "Hard to say. Been a dreadful dickens of a summer, which don't actual *up* any real property. But, of course, this doesn't negate a profitable sale for *you*."

The man spat. Unfolding a packet of chew, he stuffed a wad into his cheek and tucked the tobacco pouch away.

"Mayland," said Mr. Gamp, "with a situation such as the Pecks are in, news tends to travel fast."

"What kind of news? Bad?"

"Depends on whether you're fixing to be buying, or selling. You see, Learning's a small town. We're the community's only bank. More real estate than savings. Land poor, one might say. And in a little village such as ours, a buyer has to be on the inside. Get me?"

"Say what you mean, Haskell."

"Well, there's a tired old expression . . . *make hay while the sun shines*. And these days, there isn't a load of second-cut hay in the county. This means a few farms, the few that are poorly capitalized, will sink under. So, when opportunity raps at your door . . ."

"What's that supposed to mean?"

"Means this. Some clerk at our bank might start telling tales out of school. People believe gossip before they believe Gospel. Which means that maybe, in a day or two, this property just might attract a few potential buyers."

The man nodded. "I see."

"Right now, at our bank, Mr. Henshaw and I are the only ones who are privy to this information. Henshaw keeps his trap shut. Business isn't his specialty. Oh, he can cipher arithmetic, on paper, but I don't guess I would label Bert Henshaw the sharpest knife in the kitchen."

The man chuckled. "Haskell, you're a card."

Mr. Gamp pulled out a bottle. Both men helped themselves to a swig and a swallow, then it was recorked.

Mr. Gamp clapped the man on the shoulder. "Now then, Mayland, *you* are real sharp. Foxy enough to take advantage of inside information, and do it sudden, before such a fact of nonpayment leaks to the outside."

Winking, the man said, "I catch on. And I'm mighty glad you took me under your wing on this, Haskell."

"So am I."

Without another word, the two men returned to their car, started it, then drove away.

There I stood, leaning against the toolshed, wondering if I had understood everything, or even anything, I'd overheard. The feeling weakened my knees and made me swallow a nothing in my throat. No sense in telling Mama or Aunt Carrie how I'd listened. All I knew was that Mr. Gamp had fixed an eye on our home, our farm, and was trying to pawn it off to somebody he called Mayland.

For much of the day I toted water to our vegetables. More out of rage than reason. Anger, not ambition.

"I'll show 'em," I said over and over, wasting my breath as I balanced two full buckets in my hands. Out of spite, or stupidity, I refused to rag the handles. Before realizing the harm I was doing to myself, my right hand clamped into a claw. It felt wooden. My pesky fingers wouldn't open or close, and trying to ball a fist was a failure.

In the kitchen, Mama prepared a basin of warm water and sumac root. Even though I bore a few doubts about this old remedy, I went along. But not with a dose of patience.

"It's still cramped, Mama."

"Give it time."

I sighed. "But there's work to do."

"Robert," she said, standing close to where I sat at our kitchen table, touching my hair, "there's not an egg in the world that'll hatch out a chick until it's good and ready. We can't rip open a bud into a blossom."

"How long will it take?"

"Just long enough. Sit still, and I'll carve you a warm slice of corn bread. To hasten the heal."

Well, it did the trick. Even though I'm not certain if it was Mama's corn bread or God's sumac. The more I thought on it, the closer I come to reasoning that perhaps, in a way, the two were flirting cousins.

After I rewarded my mother with a hug, I went outside again to fight farming. But before I could spit on my palms, a car returned. A different one. It was Mr. Gamp. All alone. Walking to where I stood frowning at him, Mr. Gamp sort of smiled and extended me a handshake. I balked, then took it.

"Robert, I have tidings for you folks."

"You sold our place."

He laughed. "No, no, not at all. Quite to the contrary. Earlier today, you might've seen me with a gentleman, but he and I were looking at all kinds of property. Not necessarily yours."

"What's the good news, sir? I could use some."

"You missed your August mortgage payment. But never fear. The Learning Bank will extend a payment for you, to tide you people over, so to speak."

"Honest?"

"Of course. We bankers can be all heart when it comes to the welfare of our community and her citizens." He looked around. "A fine place you got here. Fine place. You'd be foolish to sell."

"Thank you, Mr. Gamp. We hope we'll be able to come through in September. Rain would help."

"Indeed so. Well now, Robert, the bank's open so I best be getting back to guard everyone's money. Thought my news might cheer you up. So long now."

"So long."

Mr. Gamp left.

Prior to returning to work, however, I hiked over the ridge to visit Mr. Tanner. He and Bess were sitting on their porch in the shade, sipping iced tea. Bess fetched a glass of tea for me. Really tasty. It had a slice of real lemon.

I thanked her and dried it out quick. Then I told Mr. and Mrs. Tanner about my two visitors today at our farm. I tried to tell Ben exactly what I heard. Then, after that, about Mr. Gamp's returning with the news of my extension.

"Why?" I asked Ben. "How come?"

Ben Tanner grinned. "Rob, sometimes a shiny-shoe downroader can be easier to see through than summer air. Know what happened? I'd guess his proposed deal with that Mayland guy fell through. So, before he fumbles a sale, Haskell the Rascal wants to ensure he's secured your parcel to grab. Plain as day."

I shook my head. "You mean Mr. Gamp wasn't telling me true? He's the president of a bank, Ben. Isn't he straight?"

Ben nudged Bess and they both laughed.

"Straight?" Ben asked, slapping his knee. "Haskell's so crooked he could hide behind a corkscrew."

Chapter

11

The rain refused to fall.

For weeks, whenever home could spare me, I'd been earning a dollar a day at Ben Tanner's. But due to the dry spell, Ben couldn't hire me anymore.

Early one morning he said, "Rob, you're a stout worker. However, with all this heated weather and no rain, there's little to do here. I may even have to cut back George's hours, and he's worked for me over ten years. It smarts to say it."

"I understand, Ben." I did. It was so plain that it was hurting Ben Tanner to tell me.

"A coupling of two evils, Rob. Drought plus a depression. Sorry time for farmers. Pork and beef prices have fallen so low we near have to give it away. Same for milk. It doesn't pay to place a pail beneath a cow."

"Over the radio," Bess said, "the news reported

that farmers were dumping their milk onto the street."

"We'll be all right," I said, "soon as it rains."

"Looking on the bright side," Ben said, "yesterday I was in the feedstore in town. Porter Ferguson is looking for a boy. Odd jobs. It won't pay much. I told Porter about you, and he's interested. Please go talk to him."

"I will, Ben, and thank you."

Leaving Ben's place, I ran barefoot all the way to Learning, puffing to a halt at Ferguson's Feed & Seed. The double doors were closed and locked. A noise behind me made me turn around.

"We don't open until seven o'clock," a small elderly man told me. He wore black arm garters, a starched white shirt, and half-moon glasses. "Seven is early enough."

"Sir . . . are you Mr. Porter Ferguson?"

"Yup." The old gentleman snorted. "At least I was when I turned off my alarm clock. And who might you be? A customer?"

"No, sir. I'm Robert Peck. Mr. Tanner, our neighbor, told me that you might hire a helper. I'm a bargain."

Before answering, Mr. Ferguson selected a key from his collection to unlock the door. It opened outward, with a creaky sound. Then he faced me.

"You're here early. I'm not open for business. S'matter? Can't you tell time?"

Still out of breath, I panted, "Yes, sir." I took in air. "I run all the way."

"From uproad, all the way to here? You must hanker a job real bad. Nobody else reports at this hour. You must be related to a rooster." He was struggling to brace a large barrel against the door, to hold it open. So I helped him do. "Good boy. You see things that need tending. You're hired."

"Thank you, Mr. Porter. Sorry, I meant to say Mr. Ferguson."

"Well?" He seemed to be waiting. "Don't you want to know how much I can afford to pay?"

"Whatever it is, I'll welcome it glad."

"Fifty cents a day. All day." He shuffled toward the rear of the store, and I followed. "But you'll work no harder than I do. 'Zat a deal?"

"A deal."

We met hands.

As Mr. Ferguson opened the back door, he was greeted by a flock of small white-crown sparrows. Papa had called them skunk birds. Their tiny heads seemed to be wearing skunk-skin caps. The birds fluttered at Mr. Ferguson, chattering wildly, landing on his head and shoulders, then flying around his small frame.

"My friends," he told me. "When you're in the feed-and-seed business, popularity with sparrows comes for free. It's a bonus."

As my new employer was cackling at his bird-sized joke, his laugh was akin to a chirp. Or a bird's morning song. I liked him.

"What's your name again, boy? I forgot."

"Robert Peck. I get Rob for short."

"Yup. Very well, Rob. For starters, fetch a rag and tidy up around the crank of that turpentine barrel. Some customers I got store-trained so's they measure their own into a carry can. One or two will drain part and slop the rest."

I did it.

While I worked, the smell of the place made my nose hum. A good aroma, a mixture of malt, rye, oats, sunflower seeds, and black rolls of tar paper. As I moved along with a rag and broom, I inhaled citronella, putty, new rope, creosote, and linseed oil, plus a few dusty bales of excelsior.

"If you chance to scatter any grain or seeds," said Mr. Ferguson, "don't bother it. My sparrows are magicians. And they'll make it disappear." He winked. "Sometimes I even spill some on purpose."

Never had I worked in a place with the music of so many birds. Everywhere I looked, a sparrow was pecking up a treat. Once in a while, a bird would relieve his bowels on the gritty floor, but the owner didn't seem to mind. Nor did I, even though I was barefoot. Being a farmer, assisting Papa for many a summer, I'd stepped in worse.

At Aunt Matty's, there was a religious picture on the parlor wall of some old saint surrounded by a flock of white doves. Who knows, he might have been kin to Mr. Porter Ferguson.

I didn't service any customers. Leastwise, not direct. My boss waited on every one personal, made change from the cash register, then ordered me to bear the grain bags to a wagon or a truck.

A lady tipped me a nickel. "Here you go, sonny," she said. "But don't spree it for peppermint. If you're wise you'll squirrel it away."

"Yes'm. I certain will."

It would be one more nickel into Mama's old teapot, and eventual to the Learning Bank.

"Them salt blocks," said Mr. Ferguson, "are all mixed up. Sort 'em out, and line 'em up proper, like soldiers. White together and brown alike. Even though a cow won't give a hoot whenever she licks one."

Straightening the big salt blocks made me sad. I'd always wanted to save up pennies, come to town alongside of Papa on the wagon bench, and purchase a block of salt for Daisy. She'd never had a one. For her, I planned to get a white one, to match her black and white hide.

Now it was too late.

No matter. Soon, because of my new job, I might save up and buy a weaned calf from Ben Tanner. Then, when she become a heifer, we'd match her with Beowolf. She'd lactate, to become a full-growed milker. And then Mama and Carrie wouldn't have to drink black coffee.

Then I remembered. At home, there wasn't any coffee. We'd run clean out of it. Mornings, my mother and aunt would be drinking hot water. They'd done it before. Gone without.

"Rob, take that chain to the back. Circle it neat beside another one you'll see there."

"Right," I said. But I couldn't lift the chain, or even drag it. That length of big-link chain must've outweighed three men. Yet I pulled at it and tugged for close to a minute without even giving it a scare.

Mr. Ferguson was laughing fit to bust. "Yup, I gotcha, Rob. It's a gear chain for a mill. Weighs better than half a ton."

My old boss was mere playing a prank on me, and wowee, did I ever tumble over it. After that, he asked me to relocate about a dozen rolls of black tar paper, which I could do right easy. It didn't bother me that it coated my hands all black, because

I had me a hunch that Mr. Porter Ferguson paid wages by measuring the dirt on a worker.

Maybe someday I'd own a store and be a friendly storekeeper like Mr. Ferguson. His extra pair of glasses was sitting on a countertop. So I hooked them over my ears and glanced at a mirror to see how I'd look. Smiling at myself, I said, "Yup."

I'd managed to move the final tar paper roll when I noticed a customer entering the store. And he stopped my breathing. This particular patron was the shop teacher, Mr. Orr, carrying his umbrella. Nobody knew his rightful age. As a youth, he might have marched in the Crusades. All I knew was that his eyesight had dimmed and he was deafer than a stump. In other words, as Jacob Henry once said, ready to sit on the Supreme Court.

Just my sorry luck that Mr. Ferguson was busy in the back, jotting figures to his ledger.

"Anybody here?" Mr. Orr hollered in a voice that had learned to whisper in a sawmill, presuming that everyone else was earless, except himself.

"It's Mr. Orr," I said softly to my employer. "I think he might be looking for *you*."

"Boy," my boss said, "attend him. I'm too busy. See what he wants, and if you don't know what it is, he won't either, so sell the old skinflint anything else. Make him pay full price."

"Me? You want *me* to wait on him?"

"Yup."

I was sure in a pickle.

"Hello!" Mr. Orr hooted to all of Vermont and parts of New Hampshire. "Anyone here to service me?"

Long as I live (which could have proven that day to be a very short life), I'll always pay homage to my favorite commodity among the entire inventory of Ferguson's Feed & Seed. Tar paper! In a breath, I rubbed my blackened hands all over my face, put on the extra pair of Mr. Ferguson's eyeglasses plus an apron, and (with white grain dust on my hair) paraded manfully forward to address Mr. Orr.

"Yup?" I asked.

Pop Orr near jumped out of his underwear. Or secretly disgraced it. Never had I seen so startled an expression. His eyebrows went scurrying toward his scalp, and his Adam's apple bobbed up and down for several round trips. Then he blinked at me.

"Yup?" I repeated.

Cupping a hand to his ear, Mr. Orr squinted at me in total disbelief. Slowly he opened his mouth to speak.

"Porter, is that you?"

I nodded, not trusting myself to utter another word, one that might pack me off to prison, or to hang. Or worse, to have to suffer shop class again.

"You sick?" Mr. Orr inquired.

Again I nodded, and then faked a disgusting death-rattler of a cough in Pop's direction. Mr. Orr could only mumble his next question.

"Good grief, Porter . . . what's ailing you?"

Just before Mr. Orr, umbrella and all, went flapping like a goosed goose out the store's double doors, I gave him the medical opinion he sought. A simple diagnosis. All I told him was two words.

"Black plague."

Chapter

12

"Whoa."

Mr. Sebring Hillman, who lived just uproad from us, contained his team long enough for me to step on a wheel spoke and then to sit beside him on the wagon bench.

"Thanks, Mr. Hillman. I sure could use a ride home. I'm beholding."

With an easy looping snap of his reins, Mr. Hillman moved the team forward.

"What are you doing in town, Brother Peck?"

I smiled. "Working. Took me a job at the feed-store, helping out Mr. Ferguson."

"A decent man."

"Yup," I said.

"How are you folks doing?" he asked.

"Well, I don't guess any worse'n anybody else. You know, because of there's not much rain."

Mr. Hillman looked at the sky. "No chance today."

We jawed about weather and crops, and that Ben Tanner was healing. Mr. Hillman's wife, Astrid May, had taken a pie to the Tanners after the trouble with General Robert E. Lee.

When Mr. Hillman pulled his team to halt at our place, I was fixing to jump down.

"Hold it, Robert. Stay on. Because yesterday I found a tool in my barn that I'd borrowed from Haven. I want to return it. Would you bring it home?"

"Sure."

At the Hillman place, Mrs. Hillman heard the team and wagon, come out the house with a dish towel over her shoulder, and waved. I waved back.

Dismounting the long wagon, Mr. Hillman led the way to an open toolshed. Inside, I admired the sturdy frame of a half-built and well-grained table.

Mr. Hillman nodded at it. "Like your pa, I make our furniture. Every stick."

"It looks good. What kind of wood?"

"Cherry. Ought to look nice when it's finished and polished like an apple. Astrid May always wanted a cherry table. Sold the last one I put together. A city fellow come along and told me that

Shaker-made was top grade. Offered me a price. So I took it glad."

"Sister Hillman will be happy with this one."

"Hope so. She's a fine woman. A good wife." He looked at me strange. "You fixing to marry soon?"

"No, I'll be coming up fourteen this coming winter. I'm too young to think on such."

"Well, I was not sixteen when I wed mine. Both of us young. Growing up has a way of making a man do, instead of consider."

"How come you asked me if I was fixing to get married?"

Before answering, Sebring Hillman rubbed his hand along the raw table wood. It was yellow with dust. "Because," he said, "I was down by the crick a few weeks back, fishing. I seen you kissing the Tate girl."

"Oh. Well, we don't talk at all about anything too serious. Not about a wedding or like that."

Mr. Hillman nodded. "Come along with me, Robert."

"Where to?"

"Inside my barn. Something in there you ought to study."

We went inside.

Standing very still, Mr. Hillman looked up, then

pointed at one of the barn's thick crossbeams. "Oak," he said, "and solid as Sunday." Lowering his arm, he kept staring up at the beam, shaking his head.

"What is it, Mr. Hillman? What's wrong?"

"Happened years ago. Her name was Letty. Miss Letty Phelps. She was related to Haven. As you know, when my woman took sick, she hired out to us. Lived here. But Letty was too pretty to pass by. I took to her. And got her in trouble, you know in a family way. In pod."

I didn't speak.

"She bore a baby girl. My daughter. Then ashamed of it all, Letty drown the child. Done it just outside in my horse trough. After that, she tied a rope to that beam, right there above us, and hanged herself."

"I'm sorry, Mr. Hillman. And I remember that rainy night in the churchyard, and the baby's coffin you brung home, to here."

"It hurt to own up. Yet the shame of not admitting my sin hurt worse. Took me a while. Too long. But I did make my claim, to you and to Haven that night, and to the Lord."

Mr. Hillman walked back and forth, three or four times, shaking his head as if trying to shake an illness.

"Years back, my doing with Letty Phelps began near the crick, under those pretty white birches where you and your sweetheart were. The same spot." He looked square at me. "Forgive me, Robert, for saying this to you. I have no son. You don't have a father. No more will I say than this. To love is a blessing. But to trouble a young girl is a curse."

For a time, I stood in the barn with our big neighbor, looking up at his sober face. He had nothing further to say about Letty. When I followed him back to the toolshed, Mr. Hillman handed me a mattock.

"Here's the pickaxe I borrowed from Haven." He paused. "My excuse for luring you here to point out a beam. Forgive me. I'm either a good neighbor or a busybody, and I'll let you decide."

Before I left, the Hillmans gave me one more thing to bring home, this one a gift. It was a twenty-pound catfish. I steamed it outdoors and we ate it for supper. Not much got left for Miss Sarah, but enough. The hot white catfish meat was a real treat and offered second helpings all around.

Aunt Carrie went to bed early.

My mother and I stayed up. We sat together in the kitchen, and I told her all that Mr. Hillman had told me, things she already knowed. I figured that Mama might want to talk about Letty Phelps and her sorrow, but I was quite wrong. Instead, my mother told me things I didn't know, or never suspected.

It was about my sisters.

"They all married young," Mama said. "So very young. Fourteen or fifteen, no older than that. All four before they'd turned sixteen."

"Why did they?"

Mama looked at me. "For their babies. To give their little ones a family name other than Peck."

"You mean . . . it was Mr. Hillman?"

Mama shook her head. "No, Robert, it certain was *not* Sebring Hillman. But your sisters were pretty. As fair as Becky Tate. And in trouble."

"Are you worried that Becky and I . . ."

"No. But both of you are yearning young. She's a lovely lass, your Becky Lee, hair blacker than a raven's wing, and eyes that dance with the Devil."

"She's a nice girl."

"So were your sisters. All nice. Clean and respectful. I guess what I'm trying to say is this. Since your father left us, you've growed up so quick, and so sudden. Up until Pinky died, you were only a boy. Lately, you seem so much taller and stronger.

Close to becoming a man." With her elbows on the kitchen table, my mother rested her chin in both hands and stared at me.

"Mama, I'm tired. Today I got told too much to contain. More'n I can carry." I touched her face. "But I'm also old enough to think, to reason, and do right. Trust me."

"I do."

"Good."

I clinked my nickel and both quarters, my day's pay, in the teapot and replaced its little lid. It seemed so empty. Perhaps the pot only longed once again to hold tea. Yet there wasn't a leaf of it in our pantry.

Mama kissed me and then tiptoed quietly up the creaking stairway to her bed.

I stayed up, walked outside, and studied a creamy three-quarter moon. After all I had heard today, the moon prompted me to a promise, to swear a secret oath.

"Never will I trouble a girl."

Chapter

13

It was September.

There wasn't a second cut of hay. And very little of our field corn could I cut or try to sell for silage. The ears were few and stunted, yet I collected every one to shuck for our chickens.

During warm weather, our hens roamed free, surviving by pecking at every bug and beetle. Winter was another story. The snow and cold demanded that our chickens would stay cooped. Corn had to be provided. An animal, even a hen, burns more fuel in winter. So do people. This meant that our teapot money drained away to vacant.

Mama and Carrie canned every vegetable that I could dig up from our little backyard garden. Not much to can. In better years, my mother and aunt would spend weeks by the stove, paring, slicing, and processing all their jars on our Acme American stove.

One time, sweaty with boiling beets, Mama said to her sister, "There be only two seasons in Vermont. Winter and canning." Mama had a wit.

At least I kept my job at Ferguson's Feed & Seed. During my noon hour, on the first day of September, I made a trip to the Town Clerk's office. A lady was there. The only person.

"How do," I said, taking off my hat. "My name is Robert Peck. Me and my family, we're uphillers. Is this where people pay taxes?"

"You're here for that purpose?"

"Yes'm." I swallowed. "No, because I don't have the thirty-five dollars. Not a penny of it. My father died, and . . ."

"What's your name again?"

"Peck."

She searched through her records, then stopped. "Haven Peck?"

"No, I'm his son. He's dead. Please, tell me what happens if I can't pay."

"Then your property is placed in jeopardy. Perhaps you ought to consult a lawyer. My brother-in-law happens to be . . ."

"Excuse me. I want to be polite, but we don't have a lot to spend, on anything."

"Are you employed?"

I nodded. "Yes, a regular job at the feedstore, right here in Learning. If you doubt it, you can ask Mr. Porter Ferguson."

"How old are you, young man?"

"Thirteen. Does that make a difference?"

"Not usual. I was just curious. You'll have to register for school in two days. And attend. You won't be working any longer. By the way, what was your stipend at the feedstore?"

"My what?"

"Pay. What do you earn?"

I smiled at her. "Well, I started there at fifty cents a day, but because I come early and stayed late, Mr. Ferguson upped my wage to seventy-five cents."

"Six days a week for Mr. Ferguson?"

"Yup. I mean yes'm."

"Do you own your farm outright, or is there some sort of a lien or mortgage on it?"

"It's mortgaged. But we've been paying it off pretty steady. Only four years to go and it's all ours. Free and clear."

The lady made a note on our paper.

"Your property will not be free and clear if you haven't settled your annual tax. How do you propose to raise thirty-five dollars? Or do you expect to become a burden to the township?"

"No, I don't."

"By statute, there is a fiduciary obligation on indebted real property. Legally, no continuant can be considered in our jurisdiction without further proof of viable assets. An attorney, for a reasonable fee, can explain all this to you and then represent you in court, at which time you can opt for a judicial review."

My knees started to wobble. Inside my brain, all she'd said was starting to mill around, and I didn't savvy a word. "We want to pay our taxes. But can't right now. By next growing season, in a year, I'll be able to settle whatever we owe."

The woman smirked. "If I had a dime for every deadbeat that gives me that story, I'd be rolling rich."

"Thank you," I told her, even though she hadn't given me much of a cheering.

When I returned to the feedstore, Mr. Ferguson was messing through a pile of papers. He sat with his ledger book before him.

"Few of the people who trade here are paying me any cash. What they owe's on the cuff." Mr. Ferguson shook his head. "And my cuff isn't big enough."

"I'm sorry, Mr. Ferguson. It would be nifty if you'd prosper. You're a honest merchant."

"Rob," he said, looking up at me over his half-moon glasses, "I can't afford to keep you on. You're a worker. But we're all into tough times. If business takes a healthier turn, I'll hire you again."

I felt stunned.

"Then I'm all through here?"

"Yup. I'm sorry. Hope you know it." He pointed at a ten-pound burlap sack. "So we'll part as friends, there's a bag of cracked corn. Take it. Before spring, your chickens might get hungry."

Thanking him, I left uproad for home.

When I reported to Mama and Aunt Carrie about my double dose of bad news, they both told me not to fret about it, because school was starting up again.

Mr. Ferguson's cracked corn never made it to our hen coop. Out of necessity, I fed it into our hand grinder, turning it into meal. Mama baked bread with it. Then apologized for its taste. This was corn not intended for people. But we had to live.

Just on a slim hunch, I went to visit our easterly neighbors, Mr. and Mrs. Long. Her name used to be Mrs. Bascom, a widow, but she married Ira Long, her hired man.

They had both become close friends.

"Any chance that you people might be needing an extra hand on your place? If so, I'll work hard and cheap."

Their faces told me the answer before they did. "No chance at all, Robert," said Mrs. Long. "I don't have to tell you that money's pretty scarce right now."

Ira said, "Maybe you hadn't heard. But the paper mill in town is only running two days a week. Not enough orders to meet a payroll."

I clenched my teeth, took a breath, and made them a second offer. "You won't have to pay me," I said. "Not in cash. Because I'm willing to work for food." I looked at both of them. "Please, just for something to eat. If you kill a hog, I'll help, if you give us the hoof meat."

Mrs. Long and her husband looked at each other, then back at me. "I believe," she said, "we might take you on, Rob."

Ira nodded. "At least at day's end," he said, "you'll be able to tote home a few goodies. It's a deal."

He shook my hand.

"However," Mrs. Long said, with a smile on her pleasant face, "we can't allow you to skip school. It wouldn't be right, would it, Ira?"

"No indeed. Our bargain is for Saturday only."

"All right," I said. "Even if it goes against the Shaker faith, I'll work Sunday, too, if need. Or during the week. If you can light a lantern in the barn, I can tackle night work. Any dirty job you don't aim to do, I'll handle."

Ira smiled too. "You know," he said, "before today, I don't guess I ever realized that manhood comes in a pint size."

Mrs. Long said, "Robert, I took a pair of pies out of the oven about half an hour ago. Would you please do me a favor?"

"Yes'm."

"Wait right there."

She left for the kitchen. In a breath or two, she returned, carrying an entire pie. And for me, a glass of milk.

The fresh smell told me what pie it was.

"Blueberry," I said.

"You got a nose," Ira said and pretended to punch my shoulder. "You ought to been born a coonhound."

I laughed. So did the Longs. It felt good. Strange, but I hadn't been laughing much of late, and it was a righteous joy to turn it loose. It was as though I had a mouthful of wrens that wanted to fly free.

"Your mother's a good cook, Rob," said Mrs.

Long. "So I'd value your family's opinion of my pie. Because I might enter it at the county fair next week."

Mrs. Long, on a second trip, brought three plates, a knife, and three forks. She cut the pie into six, and we ate a half of it, three generous slabs. I sure didn't need much urging to attack my share. If my appreciating was the favor Mrs. Long wanted, I was certain willing to grant it.

Ira and I held our forks like people do at home. Knuckles up. But his pretty woman held her fork a odd way. Knuckles down. There was no understanding female folk.

We finished our pie. I wondered if my mouth had turned as blue as Ira's.

He asked, "Rob, did you hear about the boy in Learning who ate a entire blueberry pie, all six pieces?"

"No," I said, "what happened to him?"

"Well, he went to a dog show, yawned, and took third prize."

We all hooted at that, even though I'd heard it from both Papa and Ben Tanner. But old jokes are as good as old friends. However, inside me, I was feeling guilty that I had eaten blueberry pie while my mother and aunt had none.

"Dear, dear," said Mrs. Long, "that other pie is

only going to spoil rotten, and I'll have to throw it out."

"The hogs'll eat it," Ira said.

"Or," said his wife, "I might bury it out in the garden. You know, to help fertilize my petunias."

The two of them were winking at each other, and I was a bit slow to catch on. Yet it was a merry moment when Mrs. Long made me carry the other pie (a whole one) back to our place.

That evening, Mama and Aunt Carrie and I took quick care of half of it. We saved half of the blueberry pie for breakfast.

Not a crumb was wasted. Nary a speck.

We pecked pie like sparrows.

Chapter

14

School started.

We enrolled in the ninth grade, which meant that I'd grunted myself as far as high school. Yet I was proud of it.

Becky Lee Tate was there, talking to the popular town kids. Some girls were hugging each other. When she spotted me, however, she come to me, smiling, and hurrying my heart.

Becky touched my hand.

"All those others," she said, "are talking about the pleasures they had this summer. And their vacation trips. I realize how *you* spent your summertime. Worrying, in dirt and sweat and dung. None of them will know how you worked. But I do."

"Thanks," I said. "You're different than so

many of your friends. That's why I like you so much."

Becky almost whispered. "You do?"

I nodded. "A whole bunch."

That's when she did it. Arms around my neck, Becky Lee gave me a quick squeeze. Close as courting.

As she returned to chatter with a group of her girlfriends in the hall, one of the girls said something that I happened to overhear. "Becky, how could you smooch *him?* He always smells of cow."

Becky said, "Rob smells of hard work."

Turning, she walked away.

That evening, after Mama and Aunt Carrie had gone upstairs, I wrote another poem, as I had promised Miss Malcolm I'd do. It was about Becky. Yet I knew it was too private to show to Miss Malcolm. Or even to my girl.

> *Oh, Becky Lee, sweet Becky Lee.*
> *I gather dreams of you and me.*
> *Dreams awake. And dreams asleep.*
> *Memories I'll ever keep.*
> *Of Becky Lee.*

After printing my poem, I wondered where I'd be next spring. Wishing the winter to pass, I closed my eyes, pretending it was May again.

In our little orchard, where my father had been buried this past May, an old apple tree stood by itself. All alone. Its apples were always our best, red candy in October. But in spring, the blossoms on this tree seemed to flood the entire sky with color and fragrance. And come May, I'd take Becky there. We'd stand beneath the cloud of blooms, and I'd shake the tree, gently, to allow pink and white petals to fall on her freckles and her raven hair. Then I'd kiss each petal, so she would cherish all we had together. Our discovery. I'd save my softest kiss for her heart.

September passed.

October come blaring like a brass bugle, with its golden yellow leaves, and the ruddy reds and russets of autumn maples. And again, I wrote another poem, this one for Mama; of all the months, October was her very favorite.

> *October, October,*
> *How red is your gown*
> *As you gracefully waltz*
> *With your coppery crown.*
>
> *November, November,*
> *Blankets the floor.*

The last waltz of crimson
Is waltzing no more.

I smiled, because Aunt Matty, my favorite dancing teacher, would have liked it.

While reading the poem over to decide whether or not it was fair enough to share with Miss Malcolm, I concluded that it was. For a fellow who couldn't dance a dip, it did whirl.

Next day, I sort of hung around after school so I could show my poem, which I titled *The Last Waltz*, to my English teacher. Miss Malcolm was sitting at her desk in Room 23, going over a few papers. The room was empty of students.

"Here," I said, handing it to her. "It's for my mother, but I'd like you to read it. Please."

"What is it?"

"A poem."

She read it and then read it again.

"Is the poem all right?"

"Yes, it's really all right."

"Thank you." I paused to think about what to say next. "I wanted to please you, Miss Malcolm. Even though I don't natural cotton to some of the stuff in class."

"Do you know what push-ups are?"

"Sure. We do those in gym."

"Robert, your poems are the push-ups of prose. Every poem you write will strengthen the muscles of your soul and spirit." Miss Malcolm sighed. "I'm three times your age. Maybe four. Yet I have always hoped to discover an unlit candle, ready to give light to his or her life."

"Me?"

"Yes. Regardless of your family's misfortune, Rob, resist looking over your shoulder. Your life lies ahead." She stood. "Ah, I know. You kids look at me, seeing me as I am . . . Mabel Malcolm, an overweight unwed spinster who torments you with Shakespeare."

"No, that's wrong. You're . . . well, you are sort of a friend. Even if you are a teacher."

Miss Malcolm laughed. "Thank you," she said. "And I shall be thankful for having taught *you*, for being able to lift you above manure. I don't give a hoot if my class cottons to Shakespeare. I'm going to assign it. Hear me?"

"Yes'm."

With her back to me, Miss Malcolm was looking out of her window, as though I wasn't even there. "My class is going to read Bacon and Burns, then a bit of Keats, Shelley, and Milton. Perhaps a dose of Homer."

"Homer who?"

"He is merely Homer. He's not a baseball player, but an ancient poet who scribed the adventures of warriors, Greek and Trojan. You unwashed rascals are also going to meet Plato, Aristotle, Socrates." She turned to confront me. "Is that clear?"

I nodded.

Pointing a finger at me, Miss Malcolm continued. "For years, I've taught school in this town. I was born near Learning. And I'll die here. Until then, you kids are going to bathe in the best I can provide. If you don't like it . . . tough."

Listening to her, I was tempted to remark that *As You Like It* wasn't, compared to hauling cow dung, my favorite. Yet I didn't quite dare. Miss Malcolm, I was now deciding, was sort of boiling over, like a teakettle, so I weren't about to yank her off the stove. I'd let her run wild.

She quieted some. "Robert," she said, "we teachers in this community know our job. Students here are the daughters and sons of mill workers, lumberjacks, farmers, and . . . and of men who killed hogs. So it's our mission to give all of them a few detours, if you will, into the minds of people like George Eliot."

"Who was he?"

"He," she said, "was a woman."

"Oh."

"A very talented lady who'll inspire you and perhaps point all of you into culture, and brainy adventure."

"Her name was . . . George?"

Placing her hands on her hips, Miss Malcolm said, "George Eliot was her pen name. But that doesn't really matter."

I shrugged. "Not to me."

Taking a deep breath, my English teacher let out a long heartfelt sigh. "I just go on and on," she said. "Pardon me, Rob. You don't really deserve to be the target of my frustration. All I know is this. I'm going to inflict, or infect, all of you with the most gifted writers I've encountered. Robert, I'm your manure. Fertilizer. Boy, I'll make you *grow*."

Standing there in the echo of this empty class-room, I sudden felt aware of what Miss Malcolm had been efforting to tell me. To sum it all up, it meant that we were going to grow more than just taller.

In a way, Miss Malcolm, although she might not know it, was really a farmer. She was determined to plant seed. As for harvesting, that would be ours to reap. Looking at her, I was seeing more than a teacher. She was, in her way, a soldier. Or one candle. Her enemy was our darkness.

"You're a good teacher, Miss Malcolm. All the kids say so. We're lucky to have you." Glancing down at my feet, I said, "Even though I don't say it right."

She smiled. "You said it with violins."

"I have to go now. But I just wanted you to read my poem on October. So you'd see that I'd kept a promise."

"Will you write any more?"

"Yes'm. If you'll read the ones I write." I paused. "And, even if you won't, I'll still keep on writing. Not for you, Miss Malcolm, because I'm sort of making them up for me."

"Good." She touched my shoulder. "Create to please yourself. Allow each little poem to be a secret song."

"I will."

All the way home, I tried to remember everything that my favorite teacher had told me. Things like the fellow called Homer was maybe too poor to afford a last name.

My body was changing. In many ways. All the sweating chores and fieldwork that I'd done had hardened me. But that wasn't all. Writing poems made me stouter. Yet it wasn't this that was pleasing me. I knew. Poetry was a pillow on the hard bed of life.

Poems, and a teacher like Miss Malcolm.

Chapter

15

I worked for Ira and Mrs. Long.

The vegetables I brung home were sore needed, yet our November supper plates were skimpy. But we final had milk. Thanks to Ira's cow, a half-gallon jug a day.

Ten days ago, Ira butchered a hog. He give me the head to carry home, and Mama boiled it for a stew.

I'd also made a few trips to Mr. Clay Sander's place, where Papa had worked so many years. I asked him for work. Though he couldn't hire any more hands, Mr. Sander give me a few meat scraps. He was a good man.

"When times get better, Rob," he said, "if you want, you'll have yourself a job here."

Every week, Becky would bake some goodie,

bring it to school, and sneak it to me. Once I was too hungry to thank her. I just wolfed it. To look at me, Becky said, made the snowy weather seem colder. She also brung me gloves and one of her father's old coats . . . a bit too large, because of my size and weight loss, yet it felt welcoming warm.

On Thanksgiving, even though turkeys were cheap, we didn't have one in our oven. There was no school. Early that morning, I raided our chicken coops, disturbing all the clucking matrons, found the plumpest hen, and twisted her neck to a crack. After plucking her feathers, I chopped off the head and feet, and pulled the bowels. Her warm guts steamed on the snow. They didn't waste. I tossed them to the other chickens to fight over.

You can't roast or stuff an old hen, so Mama cut it up and boiled it slow. It chewed as tender as a truck tire. But nobody complained.

Ira stopped by. "If you want to go deer hunting, be at my place at five o'clock tomorrow morning. We'll go up mountain and be in the woods an hour before light."

"All I got is a twenty-two rifle."

"Forget it. I got extra, a Winchester for me and

a Savage for you. And cartridges. For deer we won't spend many. They never tarry to hear a second shot."

On Friday morn, I was up at four, pulling on wool. Three sweaters under the coat Becky give me. For breakfast, I gnawed on the chicken neck, ate the gizzard, and then skinned a wrinkled potato, which I ate raw. I copied that trick from Papa, recalling how he always called potatoes our *earth apples*.

Carrying rifles, Ira and I started up mountain, hiking silently through moonlight and snow. Cold and clear. Good weather to stalk deer. The leaves were off the trees, lying wet and brown beneath the early snowfall, and wouldn't betray us with a rustle.

Deer are night browsers. Rarely will you spot one in daylight, regardless of how much bark and buds are around to eat. They'll also go for willow like a moose.

Two days ago, Mr. Lampson Henry (father to Will and Jacob) shot a buck. Twelve antler points. Yet, after yesterday's tough hen, I'd settle for a young deer; a spike, or a forkhorn. Lighter to drag and softer to chew.

Walking uphill and trailing Ira, I whispered to

him. "I don't have a hunting license. They cost a dollar."

"No mind. Neither do I. Our government hasn't prohibited eating yet. Only drinking." He turned to me. "No more chatter. In woods, a mouth is foolish, but an ear is wise."

I kept mum. We climbed higher. Despite the cold, my body started to sweat. A Savage is a heavier tote than a squirrel gun.

Still dark. In Vermont, a late November sun takes its time to awaken. Days are short workers. The darkness would help us. Dawn has a way of prompting deer to bed down.

Ira stopped.

Bending, his gloved hand brushed the snow in front of his boots. Deer tracks. The twin points of a delicate hoof had left clear prints. Nearby, I saw deer droppings. Yanking off a glove, I touched the black pellets, feeling warmth. Fresh, only minutes old. Ira also felt it. Then he gestured to me that where we stood, right here, was far enough.

In a forest, a hunter can't hurry to overtake a deer. The only method is to wait until one walks his way. Patience is more than virtue. It's venison.

Stooping again, I noticed only a single track.

One deer. This be odd. A deer is seldom a loner. They travel in herds. One buck, a few does, and yearlings. At this time of year, no fawns. By winter, an early spring fawn had become a yearling, not fully growed, but staying close to a doe.

Ira hadn't budged. He stared at one spot, listening. His eyes never twitched.

We waited. Earlier, while climbing, our breath feathered out into the cold in large puffs. No longer. Our breathing clouds were smaller, coming easier and less often.

Hard to measure how long we stood as stones. Luckily, the wind was in our faces. Ira had made sure of this. Had it been to our backs, our scent would have told a story to the deer, and they smell a human over a mile away.

One time, alone, I had seen a panther (a mountain lion) stalking a snowshoe hare, keeping herself downwind from her prey. Snow blew into her face. More than snow. A smell of fresh meat. Those big hares number many in late autumn, a time when they are brown. Winter turns them white, for protection. Yet, come spring, there are few still alive. Panthers, bobcats, lynx, foxes, and wolves have fed well.

A friend of my father, Mr. Early Pardee, called snowshoes *the bread of winter*.

Ira's repeater startled me. He was levering a round into the chamber. My Savage was a lesser gun, a single-shot bolt-action model. So I'd already fed it a cartridge. I released the safety catch.

Raising his barrel slowly, Ira almost appeared not to move. Yet inch by inch, the rifle became level. Ready to strike. I raised my Savage.

Seeing nothing, I heard motion. A run, made by feet, and moving our way very rapid.

A dog barked.

A second later, a doe sped at us, leaping, bounding, darting past Ira and me, far too fast for a human eye to follow. Ira held his fire. But I didn't. I aimed and jerked the trigger.

As my rifle cracked, a dog appeared out of the snowy blackness, ignoring Ira and me. Ears back, he pursued the deer. Even before firing, I knew I'd missed. When the gun kicked my right cheek, nothing moved ahead of the bead on my forward sight. Empty woods. The doe had gone, vaulting high bushes and disappearing, showing me nothing except the white flashing flag of her tail.

"Missed," I said.

"I'm glad," Ira told me. "You'll sudden see why."

Ahead, where the dog and deer had come from, there were noises. Loud footsteps, as though the owner of those feet cared little to remain unheard. Someone was hurrying hard and breathing harder.

When he broke through the brush, I saw a giant of a man. Black floppy hat, a gray beard that was thick and curly. His clothes seemed to be torn rags, bound to his bull of a body by loops of frayed rope, or rawhide. His gun was a monster. An extra-long barrel. The hole of its muzzle stared at me.

Eyes burning, the woodsman studied Ira. "Who be you?"

"My name's Long. We live downroad a way." Ira talked in a calm and gentle voice. "Are you Mr. Yaw?"

"I be." He took a breath. "You the one?"

"No," said Ira. "It was a boy's mistake, Mr. Yaw. We're sorry. The lad's only thirteen. He doesn't yet know better."

Mr. Yaw glared at me, then back to Ira Long. Filling his lungs, he growled, sounding more beast than man. Pointing at me, he spoke to Ira.

"Tell him. Tell him good."

He spat. Saying nothing else, the large man turned and vanished almost silently into the woods, melting away like smoke. We saw no more of him, or the dog, or doe.

Unblinking, I forced myself to breathe, realizing that between my legs, my pants felt wet.

Ira patted my shoulder. Just once.

"Rob," he said, "let's go home."

We started down the mountain.

"After your shot," Ira explained, "and that dog barking and hounding, there wouldn't be a deer around these parts within a hundred hollers."

We walked near a mile. And I final worked up the gumption to ask Ira a question. "Who was that creepy man back yonder?"

Ira said, "His name is Shadrack Yaw."

"You told him we were sorry. How come?"

"Well, let's put the boot on the other foot. If that deer was ahead of *my* dog, or *your* dog, or anybody else's dog, Mr. Yaw wouldn't shoot. Not even a one time."

"I don't understand."

"Now listen up. Mr. Yaw is a mountain man. To him, and to every one of his kin, the three dozen Yaws in these woods, it wouldn't be right. Or polite. You broke a rule. So you best master this, and honor it." Ira paused. "You never cut down on meat that's run ahead of another man's dog."

"I guess I did wrong."

"Mr. Yaw forgave you, Robert. But remember this day, the Friday after Thanksgiving of your fourteenth year, and be thankful."

"Why?" I asked Ira.

"Because you come so close to dying."

Chapter

16

Will Henry cornered Jacob and me.

We were at school, standing in the hall by a drinking fountain that bubbled water all the time.

"You guys ought to do it," Will said.

"Why?" asked Jacob. "Rob and I don't have to take shop anymore. We're high-schoolers now, like you."

Jacob's older brother said, "That's the point. A sorry to Mr. Orr would only be a bootlick if you still had him as a teacher. But you don't. So your apology might make you men, instead of bad little boys."

Jacob said, "You think you're so growed up just because you're a senior."

"Becoming a senior has nothing to do with it," Will told his brother. "To grow up is to stand up.

Manly. Instead of sneaking around to stir up mischief. I won't make you do it. Nor will anyone else." Will shrugged. "It's up to you." Turning, he walked off to class.

"Will's right," I told Jacob.

"Are you on *his* side?"

"No, your brother's on *our* side. Truth is, the prank we played on Pop Orr a year ago is still pestering me."

"Honest?"

"Yes. So if you won't come along, I'll work up my courage and go down to the shop lonesome."

"I'll go, Rob." Jacob grinned. "I can't abide thinking you've got more guts than me."

"Let's go."

"Now?"

"If we don't face at him sudden, we never will."

We went, and found Pop Orr alone in his basement shop. Broom in hand, he was sweeping up some wood shavings and sawdust.

I said his name. "Mr. Orr?"

He didn't seem to hear. But then he squinted our way, looking surprised, and dropped the broom.

"You two," he grunted.

Doubting that Jacob Henry would do the talking, I waded right in. Full blast. "I'm Rob Peck. Last year, Jacob and I gave you some grief. More than once. We come to apologize. And to say thanks for teaching us."

Not knowing what else to add, I walked to Mr. Orr and held out my right hand to him. For a moment, I didn't think he'd accept a handshake. But I was mistaken. Clasping my hand, his grip was firmer than a eagle's claw. To my surprise, he didn't let go. He held on. His fingers felt twisted. Maybe arthritis.

"Rob," he said in a hoarse voice. "Thank you, boy."

When my friend stepped forward, Pop took Jacob's right hand with his left. Then he just stood, looking old, gray, and maybe tired of teaching.

"Jacob and Robert," he said, with a slow nod of his head. "Got to admit you took me back a step." For a second, his wrinkled face seemed to be resisting a smile. "In a way, this is kind of a celebration. Now I don't mean mine. I meant yours."

Holding our hands, his grip seemed to relax, yet he didn't turn us loose.

"I'm an old man," Mr. Orr said. "My feelings

aren't important. But yours are. That's why I credit you rascals with an honorable act."

Pop dropped our hands. But then touched us in a different way, placing his hands on our skinny shoulders. Jake Henry and I just stood there in the sawdust, unable to speak a word. We hadn't surprised Mr. Orr near as much as he done at us.

Pop nodded again. "You lads probable had me pegged as just a deaf old codger with failing eyesight and a crooked spine. I know. With such a crew of cut-ups, I'm tougher than tripe. But I am pleased you came to visit. And own up." Behind his steamy glasses, he was blinking again and again. "Even a hard-boiled egg," he said, "has a soft center."

"I'm glad we got to know you better, Mr. Orr," I told him. And meant it.

"Likewise," said Jacob. "Me too."

"All right," the shop teacher snarled, "git on out of here. And try not to burn down the high school."

Laughing, we left.

Later, at English class, I was tempted to inform Miss Malcolm all about how Jacob Henry and I had gone downstairs to make our peace with Pop. A year ago, I would have spilled the whole story.

Yet I didn't. Doing it was enough. All I told Miss Malcolm after class was that Miss Sarah died. I knew our English teacher was partial to cats, and said how sorry she felt.

On the way home, I stopped by Ferguson's Feed & Seed, to say a brief howdy to my favorite proprietor. And his sparrows.

"Well," he said. "It's young Rob."

I caught him trying to shift some barley bags that were too heavy for a man of his years. So I helped him do.

"No charge," I said, giving him a grin. "This chore's on the house. On me."

I asked him how business was. His response wasn't encouraging. "Bad," he said. "A few weeks ago, in New York City, that exchange market on Wall Street took a tumble."

"I don't get it."

"All the stock fell to pieces."

"Livestock?"

"No, business stock. Shares in companies. A few banks went under. The radio predicted more might follow. I can't savvy what's happening to the United States. We used to have work. Now we seem to have lost all optimism. People are afraid of the future. Some of the local farmers tell me that they'll possible not plant next spring."

How well I knew.

"How's your family?" he asked. "Still up-road?"

"Yes, but I don't know for how long."

"Fixing to vacate?"

It pained too much to consider. So I told Mr. Ferguson that we'd stay on our farm and try to hold on. Yet I was telling myself a story. A lie. I'd missed our December payment to the bank, as well as earlier ones. Not to mention our unpaid taxes.

Mr. Ferguson went to the back of the store, and I followed. He seemed to have a purpose.

"Years ago, Robert, I used to live here. Up above, night and day. Just getting started in the feed business. Couldn't afford a house. Here, I'll show you."

Up the back stairs, he led me to three small rooms. Two were bare as bones. Empty. The third room still held an ancient potbelly stove with a black pipe leading to a vent. There was a dry sink without water faucets.

"You lived here?"

"For near to twenty years. Then bought me a house, only a walk away. Got wed. My wife died. Her name was Mildred Ann Ringgold. And I still miss her."

As he spoke, I listened with only one ear, studying the three little rooms. And thinking the unthinkable.

"It's freezing up here," Mr. Ferguson said with a shiver. "Too cold to abide. So let's go back downstairs and thaw."

"About those rooms up there in the back," I said. "Has anyone else ever lived there?"

"Nope. Vacant for years. Maybe my loft is just aching for company. A pity. A living place ought to have people. I wouldn't mind hearing voices up there at all." Over his funny little glasses, he looked square at me. "What's your opinion?"

It hit me.

Mr. Ferguson had showed me his three upstairs rooms for a reason. It wouldn't be his way to insult me or my family with charity. Yet it was checkers. He was waiting for me to move.

And I jumped!

"Sir, I could work for you free of charge. Help you through the times. In exchange, maybe you could . . . maybe you'd let us . . ." Biting my lip, I couldn't make myself finish.

He come to me. "Rob," he said, "maybe it's time you growed another inch." He poked my ribs with his finger. "Stopped in at the bank today. Talked to Henshaw and Gamp concerning a few of my own business matters. A few places are going under here in town. And a farm or two. The bankers are worried sick. They're scared skinny." He paused. "Robert, a frightened man will panic and do desperate." His voice softened. "Forgive them, boy."

"You learned something today," I said, my voice shaking.

"Yes. Be prepared to pull up stakes."

"I don't know what's left to do. It's our farm. Papa's buried under it. So are my brothers. And other kin. That place is our home."

Mr. Ferguson wiped his glasses. "Son, home is where you're cozy close to kinfolks. It isn't land, or timber, or fancy furniture. You Pecks are people, not trees. An oak might be deep rooted. Maybe, because of a squirrel, its acorn could sprout and prosper a mile distant."

"Sir, you certain are a friend."

"So are you. Perhaps you and your family want to make other plans. If so, don't worry about hurting my feelings. But I still wouldn't mind a willing helper. One that's handy and nearby. Oh, and rent-free."

"I'll let you know, Mr. Ferguson."

"By the way," he said, "you ought to pay call to the Learning Bank tomorrow. I know Mr. Gamp wants to explain matters. Best you go there and listen." He paused. "As to my upstairs offer, there's no hurry. It's waited a lot of years to turn useful again. A few more weeks or months won't bother."

On the way home, walking uproad on the packed snow of the gravel road, I was trying to plan how I would inform Mama and Aunt Carrie about the bank business. No easy job. But, sure as Sunday, I'd be stout enough to hold us together.

Fists clenched, I walked into winter wind.

Chapter

17

In school, it was impossible to concentrate.

Although I was trying my best to learn, my mind was in commotion, rumbling like a threatening storm. All I thought about was one worry. Our farm.

Becky Lee Tate brought a extra-size noon bag, as she often did, then politely claimed that her appetite was off feed. We both realized the ruse to stuff food into me. Yet we didn't discuss it. Becky refused to be thanked. Nevertheless, I ate in silent gratefulness.

As we sat together, I couldn't talk to her. My mind wasn't at school. It was home. Without closing my eyes I could see our little orchard. Four trees and four graves: A cousin. My brothers, Charles and Edward. And my father, Haven Peck.

How would I tell Mama and Aunt Carrie that

we could no longer hold the land that held our dear?

"Thanks to you, I didn't fail at school. But since Papa died, I certain did as a farmer."

Becky took my hand.

"Nobody's a failure at thirteen," she said. "Allow yourself a chance. Even if you might have to give up farming or lose the place, it doesn't mean you stop living." She paused. "It makes poor sense to burn all your woodpile before the weather quits at winter."

"Today," I said, "might prove to be tougher than I am."

Then I told Becky Lee about what I was having to face after school. Going to the bank. Hoping I'd be man enough to handle matters.

"Walk in tall, Rob. A bank is only a building. Hold your head up high and be the gentleman you always are." She poked my ribs. "Well, almost always."

My last period was a study hall, supervised by Miss Malcolm. Explaining that I had important banking to do, I asked her to be excused early.

"Go," she said, "and be Ivanhoe."

After leaving the school, I got to appreciating all of the good people I'd come to know. So many.

Their faces appeared, smiling, one by each. Wealth, I was concluding, wasn't money. Losing friends would be more painful than losing a farm.

Inside the bank, I yanked off my wool mittens and hat, then asked a woman at the first desk if I could please see Mr. Gamp. I give her my name.

"He's very busy," she said. "Do you have an appointment?"

"No, ma'am. Not really. But . . ."

"Then I'll take your telephone number." She smiled. "As soon as Mr. Gamp has a vacancy in his schedule, we'll contact you."

"We don't have a telephone. Our place is over a mile uproad. I go to school weekdays, and it don't recess before the bank closes at three o'clock. Please let me see Mr. Gamp. He wants to see me. Just yesterday, he told Mr. Porter Ferguson that I ought to stop by here."

"Well . . . all right. You wait here, young man, while I go back and check to see if Mr. Gamp is available."

She marched away. A minute or so later, to my surprise, Mr. Gamp returned with her, extended a hand, and then guided me to his office.

"Please have a chair," he said.

We both sat.

"Robert," he said, "in the past, you and I have had a few unpleasant meetings. Today will be one more."

Right then, I wanted to leave. Jump out of his big leathery chair and escape out the door.

"Believe me," he said, "I take no personal pleasure in any foreclosure. Unfortunately, a bank is often the instrument that separates a family from a home. And it's worse when the home is a farm."

"Then we are going to lose it?"

Mr. Gamp nodded. "In these matters, I alone do not decide. The board does. The action we take is not motivated by meanness. Instead, it's responsibility." He removed his glasses to wipe the lenses and left them off. "Lately, I have been working at this desk seven days a week, long hours, trying to keep the town's one bank on firm footing." He sighed. "It's uphill plowing."

Recalling what Mr. Ferguson had told me about other banks closing their doors, I believed what Mr. Gamp was saying. He looked tired, and worried.

"We have a duty to our depositors as well as to shareholders. We are a mutual trust. That means that many local citizens own the bank in common. In a sense, you are one of them. If our bank fails, it would be a calamity to the entire village, to the paper mill, for everyone."

"I understand, Mr. Gamp. But I have to find out what's going to happen to *us*."

"First off, allow me to say that there's always existed a respect in Learning for your father. And also for you. During your first visit, you placed twelve dollar bills here." His finger tapped the desk. "You probably thought that I coldly scooped up those dollars with little concern for your hardship. Sometimes, I confess, I'm overly abrupt. We are in hard times. Nonetheless, our bank enjoys no pleasure in squeezing good people."

"In other words," I said, "it's a matter of choices."

"Yes. That's very perceptive. Robert, our bank has to survive. Circumstances are forcing us to act. We, as a business, can see no possible alternative. No way that you Pecks can continue to skid deeper into debt."

"This isn't too easy to take."

"No. It is not. And if you doubt that the bank regrets its action, I can't blame you. But someday, after you're fully grown to manhood, I may be no longer around. Yet there will still be a bank here, a place of commerce where you'll be able to conduct business. A bank to make loans to merchants and farmers that perpetuate a thriving community."

"What's going to happen, sir?"

"The bank is taking your farm."

"Couldn't we get some sort of a loan?"

"You already had one. That's what a mortgage is. Thus a secondary mortgage is not feasible."

I nodded. "Mr. Ferguson sort of warned me. But I guess I had to come and hear it direct."

"That's the nutshell. The land will be put up for public auction. When the sale to a new owner is approved and legally completed, equity funds will be placed in a bank account in your name. It won't be much, because it's only five acres, and the market is meager. Few buyers."

"I understand, sir."

"I'm glad you do."

Mr. Gamp stood, as a signal for me to leave. Our business was over. So I stood as well and then offered him a handshake. He walked me to his door. It was surprising when he put a hand on my shoulder.

"A lot of people," he said, "think that I'm the meanest snake in town. After what I've just done to you, I'm convinced they're right."

"You had to do it, Mr. Gamp."

"Yes," he said, "I truly did."

Ferguson's Feed & Seed was a place I had to pass on the way home. In need of seeing a friendly face, I popped in. There was also another reason for a visit.

"Mr. Ferguson," I asked him, "now that you've had a chance to consider, do you still want us to live upstairs? I hope so. We got nowheres else to go."

He smiled. "Yup. Deal's a deal."

"Sir, we'll soon be coming. Three of us."

"You'll be welcomed."

Chapter

18

The wagons come.

Snow wouldn't clog the wheels, because a fierce northwest wind had blowed the road clear. Its pebble surface was frozen, yet dry. Bare. Rock hard.

When I'd asked Ben Tanner, he offered at once to help move us. So did Sebring Hillman and Ira. Yet I was surprised when Lampson Henry arrived with a team, along with Uncle Hume and Aunt Matty in a one-horse buggy. Only the Tanners arrived with oxen.

The women helped inside.

Bess Tanner, Astrid May Hillman, Aunt Matty, Mrs. Henry and Mrs. Long had all brung boxes and barrels and remnants of wool and muslin to help Mama and Aunt Carrie pack.

Two days ago, I had cleaned and dusted the

three rooms over the feedstore. The stove, when I'd built a fire, heated at least one room. Mr. Ferguson said that he'd relight it so the place would be partial to our arriving.

I'd given away our chickens, to Ira. Only three were left. We'd eaten some. The cold had killed the rest.

I closed the door of our empty barn.

As the wagons got loaded, I felt grateful there was so much to do. Possessions, even the few we had, have a way of owning you, body and brain. With a door constant open, the house become so icy cold. No pulse.

It was like our home was nearing death.

The more it emptied, the sadder it seemed to fill with sorrow. Mama and Aunt Carrie shuffled around inside touching places. Not with gloves. Their fingers were bare, as though searching the wood and stone for something lost.

We let our cookstove go out. There it stood, silently strong, our big, black Acme American that my mother had stuffed with so much split wood and emptied of ashes. No room for it over the feedstore. But how could I ask Mama to leave one of her life's major companions? Mama and Carrie were standing there, in an otherwise empty kitchen, holding on to each other at the stove. Even though heatless, to them, it was still baking memories.

Ben Tanner watched them there.

"Too dear a stove to leave behind," Ben said. "We got more wagons than we need. If you agree, Rob, I'll porter it to our place and store it into my haybarn. When the time comes, you can have it back. Hear?"

With four big men, Ira, Sebring, Lampson, and Ben, the stove went. Mama understood. Now it would rest safe, with caring neighbors, and have a home.

But no fire.

Before leaving, Mama and I waded through the snow to the orchard, west of the house. The graves had no markers. Yet we knew where they were, beneath a quilt of winter.

"Our lost aren't here below, Mama. They're above us. A part of the sky. Someday, we will be together again. All the Peck family. Kin and animals. No bank can divide us apart. You and Aunt Carrie and I can stand without hitching."

Ben and Bess, the eldest, headed to home property. Loaded, we started for Learning. The wind was a whip. Trying to keep Mama and Carrie warm was impossible, even though I had them bundled and sheltered some under a big tarp on Ira's wagon. My mother and aunt had few warm winter clothes. They, for half of every year, were indoor workers. Not snowbirds. To them, winter was a kitchen hibernation.

Several times we had to whoa a wagon because a box or carton got winded off. Whenever we hit a stretch of ice, the going slowed; the iron on the horse hoofs made slippery footing on which to haul. But the big horses, furry thick, leaned into their collars and pulled willing. Snorting out gray plumes of breathing.

At my request, Mama and Aunt Carrie went direct to Aunt Matty's, where it would be furnace warm. I told her I'd return in a few hours to get them.

We unloaded behind the feedstore. Then up the narrow stairs, with Mr. Ferguson there to greet us all a friendly welcome.

"Where does this thing go?"

"Where do you want this?"

"How about this box?"

Our furniture looked lost. In every corner, boxes and cartons and barrels seemed to huddle without order. Nothing looked right. Yet, while unloading, I couldn't ask people to tarry while I decided where each item belonged.

"Bless you," I said. "God bless all of you. Hope someday that I can do for you like you all done for us."

They left, men and women, the wagons and horses. Alone, I discovered that Mr. Ferguson had forgotten to light a fire in the potbelly. So I did. Then I pegged beds together, my mother and aunt in one room, me in another, and unpacked dishes, a teakettle, pots, and a black cast-iron spider. A few table knives, forks, and spoons now sprouted from a large tumbler like a tarnished bouquet.

Next I undid quilts and blankets. I found towels and soap. How we'd use these, I had yet to figure, because from what Mr. Ferguson said, I'd have to haul water up the stairs by hand. In buckets. Well, it was easier than watering a cornfield.

Downstairs, the feedstore proprietor was decorating each of his double doors with a green wreath and a red ribbon.

"It's the season," he said. "Mercy, but it's cold. Below zero. That's all the festooning I intend to do. Wilbur, my nephew's boy, brung me a Christmas tree. Don't plan to put it up. Too much bother." He looked at me. "Maybe you might use it. It's free."

"I'll take it."

"Then don't stand there. Get to my house, first

one on Oak Street, and fetch it back here. It's on my back porch."

I ran faster than a pig to mash and returned with a blue spruce. Took me little time to cross two boards for a standard. Yet, once upstairs, the tree looked green but naked.

"Rob!"

Hearing Mr. Ferguson calling me, I clumped down the stairs and into the store, where the little man was stirring through a mess of dinky hardware.

"Eye screws," he told me. "They'll shine like sparklers. So will these silver washers. Sorry. Don't have any brass." He laughed. "And I'm fresh out of frankincense."

"You really are a caution," I said.

"Yup. Now then, Rob, you leave dressing the tree to me. Fetch your mother and aunt, but don't tell 'em our evergreen surprise."

I couldn't budge. "What church do you attend, Mr. Ferguson? I truly'd like to know and maybe test it. You sure are a Christian gentleman."

"I don't belong to any."

"None at all?"

"Nope. I only go at Easter. Every year a different church. This coming spring, I'll give the Methodists a try."

Leaving next year's Methodist pillar at his store, as ordered, I raced to Aunt Matty's. Mr. Hume Plover, her husband, answered my knock and opened the door.

"Come in, Robert. You look froze."

"Thank you, Uncle Hume. We can't stay."

I told Mama and Carrie that all was ready at the feedstore, hugged Aunt Matty, and hauled my mother and aunt, plus a bundle of food, down the street and around the corner. I made them almost trot, because I wasn't giving them any time to grieve or waste on pity.

Up the stairs we climbed. The stove was heating. And the town's most endearing elf was there to greet us.

"Welcome, you ladies," he said. "Welcome home."

As my mother and aunt stood speechless, staring at the spruce, I said, "Allow me to present Mr. Porter Ferguson, the lord of our manor. Sir, meet my mother and my aunt, Lucy and Carrie."

He left. But he had trimmed our tree. It was glittering with a host of hardware. Outside it was late-afternoon dark, typical December, and the amber see-through triangles on the potbelly were shining a yellow glow, as if our tree was blossoming with little tiny lanterns. So pretty you could hear it jingle.

We ate in the twinkling light.

Martha and Hume Plover were generous friends, even if they were Baptists. Nobody's perfect. Matty had packed pie and cookies, a tin of tea, cold chicken, eight apples, and an entire loaf of homebaked bread with little seeds on top. Oh, and did we ever feast.

I saved a few seeds for the sparrows.

Just after we finished at our table, I heard singing. Below, people were cutting through the alley, practicing a carol. It was *Silent Night*. There were only five of them. So I dashed down the stairs to outside, wished them merry, and tossed each singer a polished red apple.

It seemed neighborly to share with folks on a day when our family had been granted so many friends. Besides, Matty had packed us eight apples. Three were left. One for each of us. Yet I knew I'd present mine to Mr. Ferguson.

"Rob!"

Turning, I saw Becky and Mrs. Tate hurrying through the cold. Becky Lee's mother was carrying a small parcel. It was pleasing to see both of them wave. As though good things were happening.

"We brought you a fruitcake," Becky said, shining a smile at me. "And I baked it myself. You'd better like." She laughed. "Because it's . . . as you like it."

"Thank you." I took the cake.

Becky hugged me. "If Mom weren't watching," she whispered in my ear, "you'd receive a more personal present."

"You too," I told her. "Soon."

They left.

Coming inside, I looked at my mother and aunt, as they were heating water in a saucepan for tea, and said, "I never felt so rich. Or so happy."

After tea, although it was a bitter evening, the three of us bundled up best we could to venture outside and beneath a winter sky. The wind had stilled. Almost reverent. Above us, stars grew everywhere. As if God, with one wide sweep of His arm, had seeded the fields of Heaven.

The light seemed to hum a hymn.

Between them, I hugged Mama and Aunt Carrie, feeling grateful for all the harvest that had come my way to bless me. More than a heart could hold. I felt taller and stronger, as if I could leap to pocket the stars for toys.

The starlight appeared yellow and white. One

particular December star was gleaming like a new birth. I couldn't help pointing at it, so my mother and aunt could lift their faces to worship in its wonder.

"Look up," I said, "at all our silver and gold."

A NOTE ABOUT THE AUTHOR

Robert Newton Peck plays jazz and ragtime on the piano, tends nine mustang horses and two cats, and lives in Florida. He has written sixty books and twenty-four songs, created three network TV specials, and won the Mark Twain Award for his *Soup* series of children's books.

A NOTE ON THE TYPE

This book was set in Granjon, a type named in compliment to Robert Granjon, a type cutter and printer active in Antwerp, Lyons, Rome, and Paris from 1523 to 1590. Granjon, the boldest and most original designer of his time, was one of the first to practice the trade of type founder apart from that of printer.

Linotype Granjon was designed by George W. Jones, who based his drawings on a face used by Claude Garamond (c. 1480–1561) in his beautiful French books. Granjon more closely resembles Garamond's own type than do any of the various modern faces that bear his name.

Composed by PennSet, Bloomsburg, Pennsylvania
Printed and bound by Arcata Graphics/Martinsburg, Martinsburg, West Virginia